KEY WITNESS

KEY WITNESS

CAMERON HAUK MYSTERIES
BOOK 2

KEVIN ROBERT ALDRICH

ALDYS BOOKS

ISBN: 979-8-9870927-4-3 (Trade paperback edition)

For Holly, Jayda, and Taegon

1

THE SUN HUNG low in the sky, a yolk cracking into the shimmering blue sea. Cameron Hauk watched it from the slippery black-leather back seat of a hired car. An expensive, blacked-out Cadillac Escalade, cool black leather seats, as clean as if it had just rolled off the lot, but scentless. No new car smell here. That would run the risk of upsetting a passenger, and in this type of service, the passenger was god.

It was a ridiculous vehicle under almost any circumstance, but especially ridiculous in this one. Cam was alone in the cavernous backseat of the enormous SUV, with space for at least six more people to ride comfortably around him. He felt like he was in an empty prison transport, being taken from his cell to the courthouse for trial.

Of course, if that were the case, he would have been wearing handcuffs. As it was, he was wearing cufflinks. It amounted to much the same thing. Round mother-of-pearl surrounded by black opals set in 9-carat gold, the cufflinks matched his overpriced tuxedo, his impractical shoes, and his meticulously overcomplicated bow tie. The entire outfit matched the ridiculous excess of the empty SUV.

Just like in prison, at a black-tie event you're told what to wear, where to go, when and what to eat, and forced to mingle with strangers you would probably avoid, if given the chance. Events like that were a prison sentence of a shorter duration, that was all.

But Cam couldn't let himself be distracted by the inconvenience. He had work to do. The tuxedo was just his uniform. His cover. Same with the SUV. It was ridiculous, without doubt, but it was expected. Rich people, especially the kind who would come to a political fundraiser—especially one put on by a wealthy surrogate, with no hope of meeting the actual candidate—were there to be seen, to be acknowledged, to be worshipped. To fit in with that kind of crowd, Cameron had to play the part.

The tux. The Caddy. All just part of the costume.

The driver wheeled the SUV expertly through the entrance to the marina. Like every airport, which had a separate, more exclusive section for private planes, marinas tended to separate the luxury yachts from the mere dinghies of the hoi-polloi. Anything under seventy-five feet was relegated to the common slips. Cam's driver led him into the rarified air with the easy confidence of someone who knew the way, someone who had driven this path many times before. The understated excess of the car and the beefy, black-suited, stubble-headed driver were so stereotypical that the guard at the tiny white security hut waved them through with barely a glance.

Cameron pulled in a deep breath, then another. He slowed his mind, slowed his pulse, began the process of shedding himself. Like stripping off your clothes and sinking into an icy sea, only to emerge minutes later energized and alive, reborn, he let Cameron Hauk slough off, drop to a pile on the floor, and coated himself with a new skin, a new persona.

The driver stopped at the dock behind a line of other vehicles. Some were SUVs like his, others were sleek black cars or limousines, but they all carried the same regal bearing, the same sense of entitled superiority, bestowed by association with the haute arrogance of the coiffed and bejeweled individuals who emerged from them. Women in long, glittering evening gowns and carefully sculpted hair. Men in tuxedos nearly identical to each other, the only individuality coming from the shape of their shoe, the color of their cufflinks, or the comportment of their bow tie. The women were on display in events like these, in all their glorious plumage, even if it was still the men who held the power.

The driver, Jack, pulled forward, put the SUV in park, and walked around behind the vehicle. He pulled open the passenger door and stood beside it, back arched, eyes straight ahead and unfocused, like a Victorian footman. The habits of the rich may change in form over time, but never in substance.

Cameron let one more deep breath exit his body, and with it the last vestiges of himself. When he pulled in a new breath, he was a new man.

I am Paul Baker.

I am Paul Baker.

I am Paul Baker.

He stepped out of the car and buttoned his evening jacket, eyeing the security guards standing by the entrance to the pier. Like bit players in an action movie, they were dressed in black suits and ties and wearing dark sunglasses, though the glare of the sunset was already fading. They even had squiggly tan cables leading to clearly visible earpieces. These were real security guards, but they were there for show. The guards to worry about were the ones who weren't so obvious.

"I'll be here waiting when you return, Mr. Baker," said the driver.

"Thank you, Jack," said Paul with a smile, clapping him on one broad shoulder. "Enjoy your evening."

"Thank you, sir," Jack replied. "You, too."

Paul knew he wouldn't enjoy the evening. But as he joined the line of wealthy patrons strutting down the pier, examining each of them with a practiced eye, he hoped it would be a good one, nonetheless.

2

JUST AS DINGHIES under seventy-five feet were relegated to the common slips, tin cans under two hundred feet were forced to tether themselves to the shore. The truly regal vessels had no terrestrial berth at all. Like the gods in the heavens, these behemoths didn't deign to touch the earth, but hovered at anchor offshore, sending hundred-foot ferries—mere gnats beside the mother ship—to shuttle their guests from shore to sea.

As soon as Paul boarded one of these ferries, he was ushered deeper into the ship to allow more guests to board behind him, enticed along by a line of servers in white gloves and black tails, each holding a tray loaded with champagne or hors d'oeuvres, bits of cheese to lure the mice along the maze. Paul left the cheese alone and walked all the way to the far rail where he could enjoy his solitude for a few moments longer. On the horizon, behind the megayacht that would be his workplace for the next few hours, the yolk of the sun had mostly emptied, the sky quickly darkening to a husky blue.

"Beautiful, isn't it?" said an equally husky voice beside Paul. He turned to see a woman who made the stunning sunset seem like a grainy black-and-white image. Her dress was a rich gold color—the color of egg yolk. It arched over one shoulder, split over the woman's voluminous breasts, came together in a sash over her shapely waist, then spilled down to the floor, leaving one long slit for her full thigh before piling on the deck of the ship beside tall gold heels with straps that wrapped up around her calf and crossed just under her knee like a Roman empress. Her other shoulder and both arms were bare, her neck adorned with a diamond choker that was worth enough to feed a third-world nation for a decade.

The dress was stunning, but the woman's voluptuous figure was more so, and she knew it. She stood beside Paul at the rail, back straight and shoulders square, with the air of an empress, the confidence of a woman who possessed wealth, power, and beauty in equal measure. From the keen, kind way she appraised Paul as he drank in the sudden sight of her, Paul knew he could add intelligence to her list of attributes.

"Stunning," said Paul. The woman's dark eyes reflected the blue dusk, but Paul could swear he still saw the flame of the faded sun in them, too.

She held out her hand. "Melantha Woods."

A flood of warmth and electricity coursed up Paul's arm and through his body as he took Melantha's hand, her skin soft, her hand filling his like it was meant to be there and he had somehow grown accustomed to living with the lack.

"Paul Baker," he mumbled.

His eyes drifted down to her full lips, to the sultry circle in the center between them as it opened into a smile. Her teeth were bright against her skin and the dark red of her lipstick, her smile wide and arresting.

Paul felt his heart stutter as Melantha's smile reached her eyes, the sunken sun flaring in them. His chest tightened, his breath hitched, his motor function failed him until she released his hand, released his gaze, and turned to the rail to look out toward the sea.

Paul closed his eyes for a quick moment, pulled in a slow

breath, smelled the salt and rot of the sea. He could not fall for this woman. He would not fall for this woman. Not so quickly. Not again.

The hum of the engines grew insistent, then strained as it worked to push the massive ship forward. The churn of the seawater chortled against the hull beneath them as the ship pulled away from the dock. Paul felt a gentle tug against his body and shifted his weight to counteract the subtle force of the movement. What had been a soft breeze became a stiff wind against his cheeks as the ship picked up speed.

He squinted against the wind and let his breath out slowly through lips pursed like a flute player. Sanity at least partially restored, he turned to the rail, shoulder to shoulder with Melantha.

"What brings you to the party?" he asked.

Melantha pulled in a deep breath. Paul tried very hard not to notice the way her chest moved as she did so.

"Let's not talk politics before we're even on board, Paul," she said with a soft smile. "There will be far too much of that later. For now," she put her hand on his on the rail, "tell me something about you. What do you do for fun?"

"For fun?" Paul couldn't remember the last time he'd had fun for the sake of fun itself. "I like to draw." It was the first thing that came to mind. "Pencil sketches." He didn't think of it as fun, though it gave him great pleasure. It was more of a need. A compulsion, perhaps. A way to escape. But it would suffice as an answer.

Melantha's eyebrows lifted. "I wouldn't have pegged you as an artist."

"How would you have pegged me?"

She left one eyebrow up for a moment, then smiled sweetly, slyly. Seductively.

He would not fall for this woman. Not again.

Melantha let her eyes drag slowly along Paul's body from his head to his feet and back to his head. This time, it was Paul who raised an eyebrow. Melantha's smile broadened.

"I would have guessed you spent your free time trolling the internet for distressed companies ripe for takeover."

The yacht drew closer. What had looked like an enormous ship from the shore took on the proportions of a modest skyscraper up close. It seemed like a physical impossibility for something so massive to be able to float at all, let alone maneuver in the water.

Paul nodded. "That's how I spend my days. Investing," he hastened to add, "not hostile takeovers. But that's not how I spend my nights."

"You spend your nights sketching?"

He tilted his head and smiled. "Among other things."

Her lips parted once more. Once more, Paul's heart stopped in his chest.

"Well, I won't ask about the other things," Melantha said, turning away and pulling her gaze from him like she were running one soft fingertip down the center of his bare chest. "We can save that conversation for another time."

Melantha strutted away, casting a look over her bare shoulder, moving toward where the ferry would dock to the yacht.

"I look forward to it," Paul called, eliciting one more subtle, heart-stopping smile before she disappeared into the crowd that had begun to gather near the exit.

The ferry slowed and turned to sidle up beside the yacht. A pontoon bridge had been erected off the tail of the yacht to allow the guests to step safely from one vessel to the other without danger of looking the least bit foolish or unsteady.

Paul waited at the rail, letting the crush of transferring guests ease before he joined them. He wanted to be just another face in the crowd, but he didn't want too many people around to watch his movements. He needed to get his bearings, to find vantage points, hiding spots, places to make a quick exit, if need be. As soon as all the guests had boarded, the yacht would begin a slow cruise around the bay, never going as far as the open ocean—most of the guests would find that experience far too rough for their tastes, megayacht or no megayacht—but going far enough to make swimming back to shore an ordeal. And though he'd memorized the layout of all six decks on the yacht, there was nothing that could replace the real-life experience of a space to give you a sense of what was possible and what was not. A two-dimensional rendering was useful, but a three-dimensional experience sparked more ideas and a better understanding than two dimensions ever could.

He joined the tail end of the boarding group, amid several slow-moving older couples, liver-spotted bald men with jowls that spilled over their collars and silver-haired women with necks like plucked turkeys and jewels enough to distract from their age, if only for a moment. Paul smiled amiably at them as they crossed together, even offered a hand to help one doddering lady across a small gap in her path.

At his first opportunity, Paul slipped into a side passageway on the yacht. As the ferry engines fired up again and the ship moved away from the yacht and back toward shore, slowly dissolving in the deepening dusk, Paul slid deeper into the shadows himself. It was time for the real work to begin.

3

THE YACHT WAS IMPRESSIVE. There could be no disputing that. At nearly three hundred feet long, it had better be. It had reputedly cost the owner, Mr. Devin Minsk, over one hundred million dollars. He was one of those typical rich douchebags who wanted bragging rights to say that he owned the biggest, most expensive, most lavish yacht of all the yacht club douchebags. He wanted to be the Douchebag King. And with this little rowboat, Paul had to say he'd earned the title.

Until the next rich douchebag came along and took it from him, anyway.

Minsk had named the yacht Paloma, after his wife. Paloma was Spanish for "dove". Ironically, the hundred million dollars Minsk had used to pay for the Paloma had come from anything but peaceful enterprise.

Officially, Minsk owned the second-largest shipping company in the world, making him a billionaire many times over and putting him 146th on the Forbes billionaire list. Unofficially, the shipping company was a shopfront diversion for his real business. A third-generation American of Russian descent, Minsk's true calling was shipping and selling arms around the world. Government or terrorist, fascist or freedom fighter, good guy or bad guy, Minsk would sell to anyone whose bank transfer would clear. It was said that five generations earlier, one of Minsk's ancestors had sold Russian cannons to Napoleon. Illegal arms dealing was in his blood.

Supposedly, Minsk would easily be in the top ten, maybe even number one, on the Forbes list if his arms income were included, a fact that simultaneously puffed Minsk's chest and stuck in his craw every time the new list buried him in the mid one-hundreds, down with the mere luminaries, instead of among those whose wealth was so blisteringly radiant it had burned their souls to dark ash.

Paloma, it was said, had been blissfully unaware of the source of funds for her lavish lifestyle. A simple girl from small-town Catalonia, a shopkeeper's daughter blessed with heart-stopping beauty, Minsk had plucked her from obscurity and made her the fourth Mrs. Minsk one sunny day nine years earlier, when Paloma was a lithe twenty-two and Minsk was already a wheezing, red-faced sixty. Rumor had it that Paloma's blissful ignorance had recently ended when she caught wind of her husband's dealings. It was a rude shock for a woman who had founded a charity to improve the welfare of children in war-torn regions of the world. Shakespeare had compared the fury of a woman scorned to that of hell itself, but apparently he had never married a Spaniard.

Like its namesake, the Paloma megayacht was a vision of elegance and beauty. Blonde teak wood was everywhere, blending beautifully with the yacht's gleaming, white-painted aluminum superstructure. This excursion would be the first real use of the vessel, beyond a few joyrides by the owner, and every-thing still looked like it had come straight from the box. Surfaces glittered in the soft lamplight, chairs and tables were pristine. As Paul stepped through a narrow hatch and down a metal ladder to the crew deck, he could see that even the tender lockers were spotless. There was rumored to be a twelve-person submersible tethered to the bottom of the yacht somewhere. Paul wondered idly if there was still plastic wrap on the control sticks.

He moved quickly and surely through the increasingly narrow spaces, even though he wasn't at all sure where he was going. He'd memorized the deck plans well enough, but a deck plan was not a blueprint. They didn't tell you where the fuses were or the electrical mains. They didn't tell you the best way to make a quick getaway when you were five miles from shore. Paul had to figure those details out all on his own.

And so he ran some reconnaissance, for lack of a better term. Eventually, he would need to make his way to the owner's deck, Deck Six. That's where Minsk would keep his valuables, in the shade of his helipad, his own getaway plan.

But Paul knew that getting to Deck Six was just the beginning of the job. His task was not just to get what he came for, but to get out with it. In order to achieve that goal, Paul would need to do his research. And so he was, starting at the bottom of the ship and working his way up.

Despite all of the security upstairs, both the black-suited Hollywood guards for show and the real ones intermingled with the guests, security on the yacht itself seemed non-existent. Paul had expected to need to steal a keycard from one of the crew, something to open doors throughout the boat. It seemed the crew decks, at least, were not deemed important enough for that kind of security. All the better for Paul. One less thing to worry about when the plan fell apart.

And it would fall apart. That, above all else, is what good plans did. They failed. Paul had worked on his plan for months, played it out again and again in his mind. The plan was sound. The only question in Paul's mind was how it would fail. And how he would adjust when it did. Hence the reconnaissance. The more information he had, the more creative he could be when the shit inevitably hit the propeller blades.

He worked his way down another ladder, doing his best to

soften the clang of his tuxedo shoes against the textured metal. This ladder was even narrower than the first. Below the waterline, the outline of the yacht tapered very quickly to a long keel, leaving little shoulder room for minor details like ladders and fire exits. Unlike whatever glamour Paul was sure he would find on the decks above, such luxuries were apparently deemed unnecessary for the crew.

At the bottom of the ladder he finally found himself on the lowest deck, at the stern of the yacht. From here, Paul could work his way forward to the bow, up one level, back to the stern, and so on, back and forth for as long as he could, taking in as much information as possible before someone found him and he was forced to pretend to enjoy mingling with a hundred asshole billionaires while trapped on a piece of metal floating in the middle of the Santa Monica bay.

This deep in the boat, the rooms were as utilitarian as the appointments. No blonde wood was wasted down here. Down here, the deck and the bulkheads were unadorned steel. Everything still gleamed, with the same fresh white paint as Paul had seen on the main deck above. But while there it gave the feeling of luxury and elegance, here it was all business, all efficiency. There were a hundred guests on board, but it took a crew of twenty-one to serve them, and that was just to work the ship itself. It didn't include catering staff or entertainers. Paul imagined that those twenty-one crew members were more comfortable down here amid the clean efficiency than up top, surrounded by the reek of money and bullshit.

But hopefully his theory would not be tested. So far, he hadn't see a single one of those crew members, and he wanted to keep it that way as long as possible. He patted his left breast, felt the lump inside the inner pocket. His secret weapon. But he didn't need it quite yet. If he were discovered, he still had a plausible excuse. He was an over-curious guest who took a wrong turn and got lost in the bowels of the megayacht. Gauche. If Paul had been an actual guest, he would be mortified to admit such a faux pas. But he wasn't an actual guest, and the excuse was all the more believable for the embarrassment it would have caused.

Paul strode down a long central passageway. Through porthole windows in the bulkhead doors on either side, he could see neatly labeled lockers containing life jackets, emergency rafts, and other rescue gear, shut tight into the exterior side of the ship. In the next few rooms he saw more storage lockers and one room with several tanks that were probably filled with drinking water.

He came to a doorway in the center of the aisle. He could go no further without going through the door. Paul peeked through the window and saw the engine room. Two levels deep, textured metal flooring ran across the top level, forming a kind of balcony that ran down the center of the room and around the sides. Two openings were cut into the middle with ladders leading down to the bottom.

Two hulking engines, one on either side, dominated the room. From the top, Paul could see large silver ducts elbowing up from the top of each engine and into metal boxes that were nearly big enough for Paul to stand inside. It looked like a massive HVAC unit, but Paul figured it had to be something to do with the engine exhaust.

From Paul's angle, the engines themselves seemed to occupy the majority of the lower level. They ran the length of the room from bow to stern and from the floor all the way up through the holes in the balcony above. Two crew members, a man and a woman, stood below, each wearing a white uniform that was as crisp and clean as the machinery around them. Each wore headphones and carried a tablet, inspecting the engine and checking off items on their tablets one by one.

Across the way, Paul could see some kind of engineering room behind glass. It squatted in the middle of the upper deck, with access doors on either side. More importantly, through the glass Paul could see another door leading out of the engine room. That was where he needed to go.

The crew members were down below and distracted. Paul's best bet would be to skirt the outsides of the balcony to the other side while they were still occupied with their work.

Through the heavy doorway, Paul heard a muffled bell ring out, like the bell in an old-fashioned high school, telling students to switch classes. The woman below walked into the front of the sunken engine room to consult a panel that stood there. She turned and said something to the other crew member, who nodded and came to stand beside her. With both of their backs turned toward him, Paul figured it was as good a time as any to sneak inside.

He cracked the door of the engine room as quickly and quietly as he could and slipped through, being sure to shut the door securely behind him. The crew members were wearing headphones, which should have helped to mask any sounds Paul made, but he wanted to be careful to avoid detection as long as possible.

As he slunk along the metal walkway in a half-crouch, the crew members pushed a set of green buttons on the panel in front of them.

In the next moment, Paul understood exactly why they were wearing headphones. And it wasn't so they could listen to music while they worked.

With a whir and a clank, the two engines roared to life. Even if Paul were outside in the open air standing ten feet away, the sound of just one engine would have been deafening. Inside the small metal room, with both engines starting at once, right beside his ear, the sound pounded inside Paul's head like a thousand sledgehammers. His eyes felt like they would pop from his skull with the pressure, bulging from their sockets with the rhythm of the engines. Paul tasted metal in his mouth, then realized he'd bit his own tongue hard enough to make it bleed. He doubled over instinctively, his hands over his ears. They offered little respite from the noise.

Through the gaps in the machinery and the flooring, Paul could see that the two crew members were unperturbed. They studied their panel, comparing various readouts to the tablets in their hands and nodding to one another. Business as usual for them. Those headphones must have worked really well.

Pain or no pain, Paul needed to get on with his own business. Despite the chaos hemorrhaging his brain, he forced himself to stand. At least he didn't need to worry about being quiet anymore. He just needed to avoid being seen.

His hands still over his ears, he scuttled around the left side of the balcony, past the ductwork and behind the metal exhaust box, hidden from the view of the crew members. The side door to the engineering room was directly ahead of him, but there was nothing but open floor between him and the door. Nothing to hide behind. He needed a bit of luck now to avoid detection.

He got it. The crew members turned together to the far side of the room, where he'd entered, to examine yet another panel. With their backs facing Paul, he darted across the open space and slipped through the door.

Thankfully, the engine room was soundproofed. The sudden deadening of the engine noise brought instant relief to Paul's entire body. Tension drained from his body. He hadn't realized how much his muscles had tightened under the strain of the racket from the engines. His ears were still ringing, a high-pitched background sound like a hot needle in his ear, but at least his body was no longer trying to fold in on itself. Paul ignored the pain in his ears and focused on where he was and what he was doing.

The room was some kind of control center. Banks of glowing green and red switches covered the walls, beside innumerable panels and screens. Across from them, on a wide control board below the windows, Paul saw another tablet on a stand, more dials and switches, and a bank of large red buttons covered in hard plastic flip boxes. On one side was a microphone, most likely for speaking to whoever was out in the engine room, and a two-handled control stick. Could the engine room control the speed of the engines themselves? Perhaps it was a failsafe, in case the controls in the wheelhouse failed. Or maybe, like in the old movies, the wheelhouse still had to call commands down to the engine room in order to change the speed of the vessel.

Paul turned to examine the switches on the wall behind him. A dizzying array of lights and panels and knobs and readouts made his already dizzy mind swim. He scanned the labels quickly, looking for one very specific word. He found it.

Generator.

Actually, it looked like there might be three or four generators on this ship. Made sense, given how large it was. The generators controlled AC power on the yacht, which powered everything from flushing the heads to cooling the refrigerators to cranking the stereo systems. And more importantly for Paul's purposes, the generators controlled all of the lights.

He glanced out the windows. They afforded a clear view of the entire engine compartment. Paul could see the crew members as they continue to examine the far panel. Their backs were still turned toward him, but they wouldn't stay that way for long. And while being caught in a passageway below decks was easily excused, being caught in the engine room with the engines running would be a lot harder to explain.

He'd found what he was looking for, anyway.

Paul slipped through the door in the wall behind him. The whining in his ears was even more noticeable out here. The world sounded like it was wrapped in cotton balls, and Paul's head throbbed insistently. He squeezed his eyes shut and rubbed at his temples, trying to will the noise to stop.

"Painful, isn't it?"

The voice was muffled, but Paul could still hear it, deep and gruff, with a faint Russian accent.

He opened his eyes to see a pair of shined black leather boots under black pants. He lifted his head slowly to a broad chest wearing a jacket as black as the night sky, with two columns of silver buttons that shined like stars.

Paul's addled mind struggled to comprehend what was happening. He tilted his head back, dragged his eyes up, up, up. The black jacket became a stark white collar and black tie, the collar became a broad, thick neck, the neck a bearded chin. The beard was as white and as thick as Santa Claus'. But when his eyes finally found the face above it, deeply lined and weathered, with cheeks red from what looked like too many years alone at sea with nothing but a bottle for companionship, Paul could see right away that the man standing in front of him was no jolly Saint Nick.

And from the gold-striped epaulets on his wide shoulders, Paul figured he'd found the captain.

4

THE CAPTAIN CLEARED his throat and raised his voice, practically yelling in Paul's ear. "I said, painful, isn't it?"

Paul winced at the volume. The captain gave the slightest smirk, enough for Paul to know that he'd raised his voice on purpose. He knew Paul had heard him the first time. And he was enjoying watching Paul squirm.

"That's why our crew members are trained to wear ear protection at all times." He emphasized the phrase *crew members.* "I guess you must have missed that briefing," he looked sideways at Paul, "and the one about the correct uniform. Tuxedos are for guests. Unless..." The captain put one hand on his bearded chin, pretending to think. "Well, you couldn't be a guest, because a guest would never be in the engine room unaccompanied, would they?" He looked pointedly at Paul. "Would they?"

Paul figured he could play this two ways. He could slink off like a whipped schoolboy and join the mindless throng above. Or he could own his situation and milk it for all it was worth. Might be worth something, might be worth nothing. But there was no way he was joining the other guests until it was absolutely necessary.

He stood tall, rubbing his temple with one hand. "I guess I

did miss the briefing. And," he grimaced, "it is *really* fucking painful, Captain..." Paul peered at the gold name tag pinned to the man's chest. "Captain William Constance." He held out held out his hand. "Paul Baker," he said. "Can I call you Bill?"

The captain looked at Paul's hand like he'd just as soon run it through a spinning propeller as shake it. Paul could see the war behind the man's eyes, indignance battling with propriety, before he finally took the offered hand in his. The captain's grip was slow, his hand massive. It swallowed Paul's hand like a whale swallowing a minnow.

"Mr. Baker," he said, his voice like sandpaper, his eyes like ice, "I believe you have lost your way."

Paul shrugged, the whine in his ears finally dying enough for him to feel mostly human again. "Every wrong turn is a new opportunity."

"Not in my line of work."

"No?"

"In my line of work, a wrong turn is four thousand gallons of diesel fuel that are docked from my paycheck."

"Your boss makes you pay for fuel?"

"The owner of this ship makes me pay for a lot of things."

The man might have been made of marble for all the expression in his face. His voice was just as expressionless. Slow, flat, and precise.

"Still an opportunity," Paul said.

The captain raised one eyebrow. "For what?"

"To find a new line of work."

Paul grinned. The captain did not.

"Would you like me to show you to the main deck, Mr. Baker?"

"Now you're a tour guide? You can find a better line of work than that, can't you?"

The captain stared down his bulbous, red-tipped nose at Paul for a long moment, then pointed over his shoulder at a wide, curling staircase behind him, leading up. After a long moment and a blank stare dripping with disdain, he said, "I'll leave you to it, then, Mr. Baker."

The captain reached behind Paul and pulled a headset from a row of hooks on the wall beside the door to the engineering room. With a pointed stare and a theatrical exaggeration, like a flight attendant demonstrating the proper use of a seat belt, he settled them over his ears and stepped through the door.

Paul sighed. That went well.

He ignored the wide, curling staircase that would take him back to the upper decks. Instead he opened a door on the left side of the bulkhead behind it. It opened onto a metal catwalk over a pool that ran the width of the ship. Paul could see a similar catwalk on the far side.

The pool was open to the sea on the bottom. Bright beams from spotlights in the ceiling above pierced the water, only to dissipate within a few feet into the darkness. Full night had fallen outside, and even this close to shore the seafloor under the bay dropped steeply.

Along two sides of the ceiling were long, metal tracks with gears on both sides and an apparatus that looked like a metal skateboard, with several sturdy cables stretching down.

And right in the middle of the space, floating in the water and held in place by the cables, was a submarine. An honest-to-God submersible, just like in a James Bond movie.

Paul's mouth fell open. He couldn't help it. He'd heard that these rich-person megayachts sometimes had these kind of things. He'd even heard that this particular yacht had one. But he hadn't believed it.

And yet here it was, right in front of him.

The submersible was huge. It ran the nearly the full length of the space between the catwalks, at least thirty feet. The top of the vessel bobbed at the waterline like the deck of an ordinary commercial ferry, with a wide platform and tall railings for people to lean against while they gawked at the sights above the water. The only unusual aspect was a long window that ran the length of the deck, offering a view straight up from the submarine below.

There were two hatches set into the floor at either end of the deck. The one closest to Paul was open. A metal-rung ladder led down to a small chamber about the height of a tall man. On the inside of that chamber, another hatch opened into an antechamber, then through a third hatch into the main space of the sub, a long tube with glass walls and comfortable seating that Paul could see through the windows set into the top deck.

The sub looked like it had seating for at least a dozen people, with room for more if they were willing to stand. The sub was capsule-shaped, with walls made of solid, curved glass, offering panoramic views on both sides. The interior of the sub looked as luxurious as the yacht itself. With wood appointments and leather armchairs, it looked more like an underwater man cave than anything else, designed for scotch and cigars and high-stakes Texas hold 'em more than underwater exploration.

At the far end of the sub, Paul could see the control room, where the sub pilot would sit. The whole setup was incredibly elegant. The guests could easily board from the catwalks on either side. Once everyone was settled, the sub would sink straight down, below the keel of the ship, and be off. Easy in and out.

"It's an airlock," said a familiar deep, gruff voice from Paul's right.

He turned to see the captain standing beside him. Paul hadn't even heard him come in.

"Excuse me?"

The captain gestured to the hatch closest to Paul. Paul had been staring down at the sub and the captain must have assumed he was puzzling out the intricate layout of the hatches and antechambers. "We can close the inner door," the captain said, "flood the chamber with seawater, then open the top hatch to let divers out one at a time without disturbing the passengers."

Paul's eyes popped wide. "That's ingenious."

"Not really," said the captain, his mouth set in a thin line. "Just expensive."

Paul nodded slowly. They looked at each other in increasingly uncomfortable silence.

"I see you lost your way again," said the captain at last.

"It's a very big ship," Paul said. "Easy to get lost."

"Yes, it can be hard to find a massive staircase two feet behind you. It took me years just to find the gangway." His expression was less a smile than a mouth spasm, a curt, toothless curl of his lips that bent his white mustache but did not reach his eyes. "This time, I'll escort you up."

Not giving the captain a chance to steer him back the way he'd come, Paul turned and strode along the catwalk to the far door. "What's through here?" he said, opening the door and stepping into another long passageway lined with doors.

The captain followed close behind. "If I answer your questions, Mr. Baker, will you please stay above deck from now on?"

"I have a lot of questions."

"I'm not a tour guide."

"Then I can't guarantee I won't get lost again."

Paul smiled.

The captain sighed. "This hallway holds several storage compartments," he said in a passable tour guide drone, striding past Paul and pointing to the doorways on the left and the right, "as well as our laundry facilities and our waste treatment plant. On long journeys in open water, we treat all human waste before expelling it into the sea."

The megayacht literally spewed the shit of billionaires into the sea. Seemed like an appropriate metaphor.

Over the next twenty minutes or so, the captain proved to be a very interesting guide. Paul coerced him through a tour of the storage rooms and machinery on the lowest deck, a movie theater, gym, indoor pool, and crew quarters on the deck above, and the guest suites on each of the two decks above that. Despite the yammering of the crowds in the dining rooms, lounges, and open decks, and despite the captain's pointed stares and menacing silences, Paul forced the tour to continue, careful to avoid the rooms where the party was taking place.

By the end, Paul could have sworn the captain was starting to warm up a bit. Of course, he had started at sub-zero temperatures, so "warm up a bit" was a relative term. The captain was still frosty and mean. As a tour guide, he got top marks for knowledge and experience, but zeros for personality.

"That is the end of the tour, Mr. Baker," said the captain after closing the door that led to the VIP suites behind them. They stood beside the massive, curling staircase, now three decks higher than when the captain had caught Paul coming from the engine room. The staircase rose through the heart of the ship all the way from the bottom level. From the look of it as Paul craned his neck to peer up its length, it continued curling upward all the way to the top deck.

That was where Paul needed to be.

The captain gestured toward a set of sliding doors behind Paul. "The music room and upper salon are just through those doors," he said. "You'll find the other guests there and on the weather decks below."

"What's up that way?" Paul said, pointing up the stairs.

"The upper two decks are the owner's private quarters," replied the captain, "with office, library, and lounge space on Deck Five and the bedroom suite on Deck Six." Paul opened his mouth, but the captain held up one hand to cut him off before he could say anything. "You'll need to ask Mr. Minsk directly if you'd like to tour those."

"Can't you ask him for me?" Paul said. He jabbed the captain conspiratorially with one elbow. "Put in a good word?" The man didn't move a muscle. It was like jabbing a giant wheel of cheese.

The captain gaze lost focus and his brow creased. "I highly doubt any word I say to Mr. Minsk would be considered 'good'."

Paul raised his eyebrows. When the captain's eyes re-centered, his face flushed. He started to turn away.

"What about the wheelhouse?" asked Paul. "You haven't shown me the best part yet. Where do you drive this thing?"

The captain turned back and stared hard at Paul. Paul felt like his mind were being probed with a laser, like the captain was trying to read his very soul.

Well, let him. He'd never see the truth. Paul was too good for that.

And he needed to get upstairs, to at least get a feel for the owner's suite. To see what he had to deal with.

The captain's eyes narrowed slightly as he appraised Paul. He wasn't going to go for it. Paul would just have to find another way up there and wing it when he did. It wasn't ideal. He preferred to know what he was walking into before he got there. But the best plans...

"Follow me," said the captain, opening the door to the VIP suites again.

Paul was so stunned, he stood frozen in place for a moment. "Don't we need to go up there?" he said, pointing up the curling staircase.

"Civilians use those stairs," said the captain over his shoulder. "If you want to see the wheelhouse, you need to act like you work here."

He disappeared through the doorway, leaving Paul scrambling to follow.

5

Inside the passageway that led to the VIP suites, Paul caught a flash of white in his peripheral vision. A door immediately to the left was just closing behind the captain, the white collar of his shirt catching Paul's eye from under his black uniform jacket.

When the door swung closed before Paul could reach it, he could barely make it out. Even though he'd just watched it close, the door blended so cleverly with the wall that it became nearly invisible. Paul hadn't noticed the door during the tour just a few minutes earlier, and now he knew why. If he hadn't seen the captain walk through it just a moment before, Paul wouldn't have known it was there at all.

Paul pressed a thin lever that looked like an innocuous section of the wall trim that ran the length of the hallway on both sides. It turned out to be a door handle, opening onto a steep, narrow metal ladder painted white. Paul climbed it to another passageway on the deck above. The captain was already ahead of him, disappearing through a sliding pocket door.

Paul followed and found himself in the wheelhouse. He felt like he'd stepped into a science-fiction movie. Large windows formed an arc around the front of the room, giving Paul a panoramic view of the dark bay in the moonlight around them as the yacht cut slowly through the water. Two large leather chairs, both occupied by attentive crew members in bright white uniforms, sat in front of a wide, arced console in front of the windows. There were three large computer monitors arranged in front of each chair, with a bank of knobs, handles, dials, and switches in between.

Behind those chairs, another, even larger chair was set on a slight dais in the center of the wheelhouse, with monitors on either side. A telephone receiver and various radios and microphones hung from the ceiling above the chair.

The wheelhouse had the energetic quiet that forms when people are hard at work, a soft hum punctuated by the occasional beep or buzz from a sensor or readout. The air smelled of lemons and new leather. It felt to Paul like he'd stepped onto the bridge of the starship Enterprise in the Star Trek movies. With the night sky outside the windows and the stars just beginning to appear, they could as easily have been preparing to jump to warp speed as embarking on a boring pleasure cruise in the Santa Monica bay.

Even more monitors covered the back wall behind the dais, including a large screen set into the wall that showed a map of the surrounding area. Numerous yellow dots with labels showed what Paul assumed were other vessels nearby. A large blue dot representing the Paloma was fixed in the middle of the map, with a label displaying their current speed, direction, and position. Ahead of the blue dot, toward the seaward side of the bay, the map was clear. Only a few lone yellow dots moved in the open ocean. The Paloma was sailing into an empty bay.

A young blonde woman sat in the center chair, tapping at one of the screens. When she saw the captain enter, she stood and called, "Captain on the bridge." Like a well-practiced dance, she walked to the front windows and replaced one of the crew members seated there. That crew member moved to a small chair in front of a monitor along the back wall.

"This," said the captain, "is where we drive this thing."

Paul ignored the derision dripping from the captain's words.

As the captain settled himself in the center chair and checked the monitors, Paul stepped to the front windows and looked out. He could see over the VIP balcony all the way down to the main deck, where guests stood in groups of four or five under the soft lighting of the yacht. The deck angled to a point at the front of the ship. From this height, Paul could clearly see a large letter "H" painted within a red circle beneath the finely shod feet of the glitterati.

"I thought the helipad was above the owner's suite," said Paul, looking over his shoulder at the captain.

The captain raised his eyebrows in response, his expression inscrutable. It was the blonde woman who answered Paul.

"This vessel is equipped with two helipads," she said, her voice friendly but professional, with only the faintest trace of an accent Paul couldn't quite place, "one on the bow of the main deck and a smaller, private helipad just aft of the GPS array."

"Chief Officer Whitley, this is Mr. Paul Baker," said the captain.

The blonde woman didn't stand, but nodded to Paul before turning back to her console.

Paul wandered to a door on his left that opened onto a wide deck that ran beside the wheelhouse. Outside by the rail was a metal cover that looked like an outdoor grill.

"You guys cook hot dogs out there on sunny days?" Paul said with a grin at the blonde woman. She didn't look up.

"That is our wing station," said the captain, pushing himself from his chair to rejoin Paul. "There's another on the starboard side. We can control the ship from there when we're docking. Easier to see the dock from the rail than from the wheelhouse."

He pushed through the door and stepped outside. Paul followed him into the night, the sound of the wind and the sea loud in his ears. He shoved his hands into his pockets, pinning his tuxedo jacket beneath his arms to stop it flapping, squinting against wind and ignoring the sudden sting in his cheeks.

The yellow glow of the wheelhouse lights came through the windows and bathed the deck in a soft warmth, helped by lamps hidden under the bulwarks that cast subtle strips of light along the floor where the rail met the deck. As he leaned against the rail and looked to his left, behind the yacht, Paul could see the tiny lights of the other boats in the bay, much like the yellow dots on the map inside the wheelhouse. Behind those ships, the much brighter, larger lights of the shoreline lit the night like a boardwalk carnival, their colorful reflections painted across the wavering water.

Paul craned his neck over the rail to see above him. Like hulking shadows in the moonlight, he could see the GPS array, a set of large black domes surrounded by antennae and affixed to a spire fading up into the night sky. Below that was the top deck, a long set of windows looking out over the sea, yellow eyes glowering beneath the furrowed brow of the roofline. Paul saw a silhouette in the light of one window, the hourglass curves of a woman in an evening dress like a dark pupil in the golden iris. As he watched, another silhouette waddled up behind it. Thick, stocky, bulging in the middle.

"The owner's suite," said the captain.

"And is that the owner?"

The captain didn't reply, but spat over the rail, his eyes never leaving the window.

The silhouettes merged, then quickly separated. The hourglass moved away from the window, the bulge trailing behind. For a moment, before they moved out of Paul's sight, the hourglass moved into the light. Paul could see a woman wearing an elegant black evening gown with a deep, open back, one that plunged to the base of the spine, laying bare the woman's satin skin.

Then, she was gone.

His eyes traced along the windows, then along the roofline toward the rear of the ship. A thin line of white light extended beyond the roof. That must have been the second helipad.

"Is there a helicopter on the owner's helipad?"

"Not at the moment," said the captain. "Mr. Minsk likes to walk up there."

"Like Leo DiCaprio?" Paul imagined Minsk getting off on the wind and the height, imagining himself the king of the world.

"More like Superman, I think."

Paul nodded. Same thing.

He scanned the superstructure around the top deck. The sides were smooth, with no footholds or handholds he could see in the dim light, and no easy way he could make out to access the suite from the outside. There was a short deck extending off the front of the suite, and another that seemed to extend off the back, beneath the helipad. Paul might be able to climb up the front, if he could figure out how to get up without being seen by anyone in the wheelhouse.

But it was risky. Too risky. He was going to have to find a way up from the inside of the ship.

"Is there something in particular you're looking for?" said the captain.

Paul's head turned more sharply than he would have liked. He tried to cover with a soft smile and a puzzled expression. "What do you mean?" he said.

"On the tour. What is it you're looking for, exactly?"

Paul stared blankly at the captain for a moment, then pushed his hands deeper in his pockets and shrugged. "Just curious. I've never been on a yacht like this before."

The captain took a step closer to Paul and dropped his voice low. "If there's something of particular interest," he said, "perhaps I can help you find it."

Was the captain offering to help Paul rob Minsk? No, there was no way he could know who Paul was or what he really wanted. Only two people in the world knew that, including Paul. And Paul knew that the other person would never talk.

Yet it was an incredibly odd thing to say. And after being so reluctant to give the tour in the first place, now he was offering more?

Maybe he just wanted to screw Minsk over. It was clear there was no love lost between the two. But if that were true, why hadn't he let Paul go up to the owner's decks? Because he knew Minsk was up there?

He studied the captain's face, but it was as inscrutable as ever. Paul wouldn't get any answers that way. And he wasn't about to ask outright.

He shrugged again and gave the captain a sheepish look. "I'm just looking for any excuse to stay away from the party. Not exactly my scene."

The captain stared hard at Paul once more, then pulled in a long breath and let it out in an even longer sigh. His eyes drifted toward the dark sea for a moment, then back to Paul.

"Unfortunately," he said, "it would seem that your excuses are at an end. I'll show you back to the upper salon."

The captain turned toward the wheelhouse, giving a long glance up at the owner's suite as he did so. Paul glanced up after him. He saw that same hourglass silhouette at the window again.

Standing alone.

6

PAUL FOLLOWED the captain through the side door from the outer deck back into the wheelhouse. The sound of the sea stopped dead as soon as the door shut behind him. The captain continued straight through to the sliding pocket door and into the passageway. "Captain below," Paul heard the first officer call as the captain walked out. He hurried to keep up with the captain's brisk strides.

They passed several closed doorways on their way back toward the ladder to the lower deck.

"What's in these rooms?"

The captain pointed quickly at each door. "Officer's meeting room, officer's mess, captain's quarters, first officer's quarters."

"Captain's quarters?" said Paul as he hustled after the captain. "Would you mind giving me a quick look?"

"Yes," said the captain without breaking stride. "I would."

He slid down the steep ladder with a speed and agility Paul wouldn't have thought possible for someone his age. From the grey beard, the deep wrinkles, and the general world-weariness in his eyes, Paul figured the captain had to be in his late-sixties. Yet he took the ladder like a sixteen-year-old, his hands sliding down the rails, his feet barely touching the treads. Paul was in decent shape, and less than half the captain's age, but he felt like a doddering old man as he followed awkwardly behind, his knees jutting out at obtrusive angles with each downward step.

The captain was waiting when Paul finally got down, holding open the door leading out to the spiral central staircase. He gestured toward the sliding doors beyond the stairs, doors that led to the party and the crowds.

"The other guests are through those doors," he said stiffly. "Please enjoy yourself." Paul started past him. The captain stopped him with one hand on his arm. "And Mr. Baker, should you wish to explore the ship again," his voice dropped to a deep growl, "don't."

Paul stepped through the door into the vestibule between hallways, where the staircase wound its way up and down through the ship. With a glance up the stairs, he turned back toward the captain. "I tell you what. If you show me—"

But the captain was already gone, the door to the VIP suites snicking shut behind him. The old man was as quick as a fox.

With a sigh, Paul squared his shoulders toward the sliding doors. The doors were made of dark frosted glass. Shadowy shapes moved on the other side, the shapes of stuffy, dull, close-minded, arrogant rich people. He could hear muffled laughter and the clink of crystal glasses on the other side. Paul hadn't come to rub elbows with assholes, to make connections, or to broker deals. He had a far more important goal in mind.

And it wouldn't be served by walking through those doors.

A server emerged from a side door. Tall and pretty, white-blond hair with a single streak of pink pulled into a tight pony-tail that painted the collar of her white shirt with every step. She carried a small round tray with two tumblers on it, smiled absently at Paul as she stepped onto the staircase and began to climb.

Paul looked past her at the stairway. Down its curling length, a long chandelier hung in the center of the staircase. More of a glass sculpture than a chandelier, a soft glow emanated from lights hidden within the crystal. The sculpture itself was impressive, a feat of design that appeared to run the full height of the ship. How it would fare in rough seas, Paul didn't know, but that seemed like exactly the sort of thing a rich person wouldn't bother to consider. Appearances first, practicality a distant second. Or third. Or fifteenth. After all, an expensive chandelier could be fixed if it broke. All it took was money. And if it broke in even the slightest seas, so much the better. Rich people loved to waste their money as ostentatiously as possible.

Paul glanced around him. The guests seemed to be staying put in the salons or on the decks in the back half of the ship, like good little lemmings. As time wore on and alcohol had its intended effect, the purse strings of the guests would be loosened, but so would their inhibitions. They would eventually start exploring the ship. Paul needed to act soon if he wanted to maximize his chances of avoiding detection.

He peered up the staircase, trying to see if anyone was up there, but the twist of the spiral and the bulk of the chandelier blocked his view. Aside from the server whose black shoes and pant cuffs were just disappearing around the curve of the stairs, Paul knew that at least two people were in the owner's suite two decks above. The hourglass and the bulge. That had to be the Minsks, preparing for their grand entrance to the party. If they were still on the top deck, Paul could slip onto the deck below them without attracting attention, then wait for an opportunity to climb further. It wasn't a great plan. Too many unknowns, too many variables. But it was the best plan he had at the moment.

As silently as he could, Paul wound his way up the staircase, moving slowly to be sure he wouldn't catch up to the server. The steps were made of marble, with deep orange and black veins. From marble veining to patterned inlays to tabletops and backsplashes, the entire ship was decorated with a riot of expensive materials and sumptuous, intricate patterns. Like a typical

Russian oligarch, Minsk had infinite funds and zero taste. The patterns clashed horribly with each other, giving the yacht a frenetic, reckless air. The chaos of the design no doubt matched the personality of the owner perfectly.

Paul crept up the stairs, craning his neck to see around the curve as much as possible. He came to the landing of the next deck, Deck Five, one deck below the owner's suite. The server was continuing upward with her tray and didn't seem to have noticed Paul below her. Paul decided not to push his luck. He stepped off the stairs.

A room surrounded the stairwell like a lobby, decorated with a subdued elegance and a tasteful refinement that did not match the rest of the yacht. Several doors were set into the walls on three sides. The two across from Paul toward the stern of the ship were sliding double doors made of frosted glass, like those leading to the party below. The doors on either side were solid single doors.

In one corner to his left, windows in the wall gave Paul a view into an office with a desk, a small couch, and several chairs. Inside, Paul could see a man in a tuxedo behind the desk, typing on a laptop. A stab of fear ran down Paul's spine. He darted away, out of view of the window, watching the man as he did so. The man didn't look up, didn't show any sign that he'd seen Paul.

Paul slipped through the closest door, the one beside the office, and found himself in a long, narrow room that ran along the outside of the yacht, with doors at either end and windows along the far wall that looked out upon the dark waters of the bay. The moonlight painted the waves in thin silver lines, the lights of the shore winking in the distance, the scene darkened by a tint on the windows.

Along the length of the facing wall, tasteful art in sturdy, subdued frames hung below soft spotlights. That explained the tinted windows. From the fine frames and the even finer paintings, these works were clearly valuable. Sunlight through the windows would destroy them. The soft lights above them would not. They accented the beauty of the artwork, let the art speak for itself without using bright lights to draw attention.

And the art was more than enough to attract the eye. The works themselves were a mix of modern and classical styles, but all were complex and nuanced. No dogs playing poker here, as Paul may have expected from a lout like Minsk. Instead, there were tasteful nudes in the chiaroscuro style of Caravaggio or Vermeer hanging beside the colorful cubism of Picasso or the post-impressionism of Cézanne. Paul didn't recognize any of the artists. These weren't high-value originals from famous painters. But the pieces were exquisite, nonetheless, displaying a breadth of eras and styles. The narrow gallery was almost a survey of art history in just a few paintings.

The subjects of every piece, even the more surreal ones, were women. All of them portrayed scenes of anguish or indecision or deep contemplation. Though there were only perhaps ten or twelve paintings arrayed along the length of the wall, their selection showed a depth of thought and feeling that stunned Paul, stopped him in his tracks in the center of the room. Surely these could not have been selected by Minsk himself. From what Paul knew of him, the man was an oaf, as incapable of understanding the subtle connections between Goya and Gliezes as he was of understanding the subatomic physics of a neutron star. And it seemed to Paul that if Minsk were to choose a room full of paintings of women, there would be far less scuro and a lot more chiaro, with nary a stitch of clothing in the lot. And the feelings of the characters in the images wouldn't even cross his mind.

No, the art in that room had to have been selected by someone else. Perhaps by Mrs. Minsk, the Paloma who was the namesake of the yacht. Paul knew almost nothing about her. Though she maintained a public profile of generosity and kindness, she rarely gave interviews, and when she did, she kept them focused on her charity work, revealing nothing about herself or her personal life. She had come from a humble life in Spain and married Minsk as a young woman in her early twenties. And she was drop-dead gorgeous. That was the extent of Paul's knowledge of the enigmatic Paloma Minsk.

But clearly she had impeccable taste in art. Why someone with such sensibilities would marry a cretin like Minsk was beyond Paul. And what about the subject matter? Women in anguish and contemplation? The yacht had just been built, which meant it had just been furnished. Had Paloma selected these works to make a statement, some kind of cry for help, a way to express her unhappiness with her husband in a way that he would most likely never notice, perhaps never even see? Paul doubted Minsk spent much time in this gallery. There were three comfortable chairs arranged under the windows, spaced down the length of the room, positioned to allow contemplation of the art. Paul couldn't imagine Minsk contemplating anything but his next deposit of laundered money.

Paul pulled his attention back to the task at hand. Aside from the door he had entered, there were two other doors in the gallery. The door to Paul's right as he faced the artwork would lead to the office where the man in the tuxedo was working, so Paul took the door to his left.

Every door was a risk. He couldn't see through them, and they were all automatic. There was no way for him to slowly open a door and peek in to see if anyone was on the other side before he stepped through. The best he could manage was to trigger the door, press himself flat against the wall, and hope that, if anyone were inside, they would think the door had malfunctioned and be too unconcerned to bother investigating. Or, simply walk through and play the role of the innocent, wandering guest.

Both terrible plans, but they were all Paul had in the moment.

Fortunately, this door opened to another room empty of people. And full of surprises.

Instead of art lining the walls, this room was filled with books. It was a tiny square space, but there had to have been a thousand books filling the cleverly built bookcases set into the walls. The bookshelves were sectioned thinly, each wide enough for only ten or twelve books, each with a tasteful wrought-iron band across the middle to hold the books in place in rougher seas. Paul tugged on one. It unlatched easily, allowing access to the books behind.

He scanned the titles. He was no English scholar, but he enjoyed literature. The shelves were filled with classics and modern classics alike, from Chaucer to Steinbeck, Plato to Garcia Marquez, with what looked like a good helping of crime thrillers and contemporary romances from Nora Roberts, Eloisa James, Lee Child and the like in the mix, as well. Many of the titles were in Spanish, further confirming in Paul's mind that Paloma was behind the design of these rooms. Perhaps this entire floor was hers and the upper floor was Minsk's. Maybe they had so little in common that they separated their worlds completely now.

Or maybe Paul was making everything up. He knew nothing about Paloma. She'd married Minsk for some reason. Maybe she was in love with him. Minsk was rich and successful and had been handsome once. Now older, his gut had ballooned, but he still had a roguish charm to him. Maybe he had that ability, shared by so many successful actors, politicians, and business leaders, of making anyone they were with feel like the most special person in the world. Between that kind of charisma and the irresistible seduction of wealth, what young woman wouldn't fall in love?

Regardless of her taste in husbands, Paloma had impeccable taste in art and in literature. In the center of the library were two chairs set around a table, with a music player in a holder in the center. He spied small speakers hung in the corners of the room. Paul didn't bother to check, but he had no doubt the music would be just as tasteful as the art and the books.

The room had no other doors, so Paul went back into the art gallery, triggered the door he'd first entered, and peered through the doorway at an extreme angle from the side, checking to see if the man in the tuxedo was still working in the office.

He couldn't see well enough, so he poked his head out a bit more, then pulled quickly back. The man wasn't in the office, but Paul had caught a glimpse of him as he climbed the central staircase toward the top deck. His polished shoes, the black stripe of his dress pants, the white cuff of his shirt under his black dinner jacket, the hand swinging back and forth as he climbed, holding a silver laptop.

Paul hadn't seen any more than that, hadn't seen the man's face. And he was climbing up, not down. Away from Paul. But Paul waited behind the wall of the art gallery anyway, his heart pounding in his ears. He took deep breaths to calm himself, releasing them slowly, silently.

When no shouting came, when the man in the tuxedo didn't come to ask him why he was sneaking around or to demand that he go downstairs, Paul finally calmed down and thought about where to go next. The art gallery and library were only a fraction of Deck Five. Even if the entire deck were Paloma's, it was still worth exploring. He still figured Minsk's personal office was his best bet, and that was probably upstairs. But it was worth checking the office next door, nonetheless.

Paul took a deep breath and darted around the corner into the hallway, headed toward the office. He stopped, hand on the doorknob, but he wasn't sure why. Something seemed off. He could see clearly through the office windows now. There was no one inside. The man in the tuxedo was gone, upstairs. Paul could hear soft bumping noises above him, like heavy footsteps, the sound drifting down the stairwell.

But something had triggered Paul's subconscious, something that had stopped him cold. And Paul always trusted his subconscious. He took another deep breath to calm his anxious mind.

That's when it hit him.

A scent.

A subtle scent that hadn't been there before. Floral and citrus. A bright, seductive scent. Like perfume.

Like a woman's perfume.

Slowly, Paul looked over his shoulder.

Standing behind him, leaning against the far wall, bare arms crossed over her hourglass waist, an amused smile on her captivating face.

Paloma Minsk.

7

"IF YOU'RE TRYING to steal something, you've got a long way to go for a getaway," said Paloma, only a slight Spanish accent in her smooth voice. "And you really need to work on your hiding. You're terrible at it. I found you, and I wasn't even trying."

Paul sighed and let his shoulders slump. He came out of his ridiculous mid-sneak crouch and turned toward Paloma, his eyes cast down in conciliation. "I'm so sorry," he said. "Please forgive me. I'm not trying to steal anything, I swear. I'm just not much for parties, and my curiosity got the better of me." He looked up at her, and his words slowed and stacked in his mouth. "I couldn't resist... exploring... this beautiful... yacht."

Watching Paul drink in the sight of her, Paloma's amused smile became a beguiling smirk. She uncrossed her arms and set a hand on one curvaceous hip.

"Did you find anything interesting?" she said.

Paul knew his mouth was hanging open, but for some reason he couldn't seem to close it.

Paloma's dress was made of black sequins, shimmering in the soft light. The opening down the front was almost as deep as the one down the back that Paul had seen from the deck outside the wheelhouse. It plunged nearly to Paloma's belly button. And

41

her new posture—hand on hip, one long leg bared through the slit in her dress—did not make it any easier for Paul to settle his pounding heart. Instead, it sent his mind into an entirely different kind of anxiety.

He gulped. Loudly.

Paloma laughed, a low flutter that made Paul's heart race even harder. Her face was as beautiful as her figure, with full, oval lips, dark, penetrating eyes, long, lustrous black hair, and a gorgeous, dark Spanish complexion. But when she smiled, that beautiful face took on a luminous quality that redefined beauty itself. Paul couldn't understand why Paloma had married Minsk, but he could clearly see why Minsk had asked for her hand. Paloma's external beauty was incomparable. And if her taste in art and literature were any representation, her internal beauty surpassed it.

Not that Minsk was likely to care about the internal. He would have fixated purely on Paloma's external features. And those were impossible to ignore. Paul would have happily stood in the hallway for the remainder of the journey just to drink in Paloma's presence.

But he couldn't do that. He wasn't here to gawk at a beautiful woman. He was here for something much more important. And if he was lucky, he might have found himself another tour guide.

"Actually," said Paul, pointing his thumb to the side, finally regaining his powers of speech, "the artwork in the gallery is exquisite. Did you choose it yourself?"

"Why would you think that?" said Paloma, her smile fading to a subtle, teasing smirk again. She stepped past Paul into the gallery, moving with the slow, lithe grace of a woman who knows her own appeal and is accustomed to being watched, but who's also smart enough to use it to her own advantage, when it suits her.

"The subject matter, for one," said Paul, casting an eye around the lobby before following Paloma into the gallery. No one was there. Once he'd gotten Paloma to show him around, he could still sneak upstairs without anyone knowing.

"Women?" asked Paloma. "Believe me, women are my husband's favorite subject. At least when it comes to something to look at." She raised her eyebrows at Paul's surprise. "It's no secret, Mr..."

"Baker," said Paul. "Paul Baker."

"I haven't seen you before, Mr. Baker. Perhaps you're not familiar with my husband's... well, idiosyncrasies."

"Only by reputation," said Paul.

"Reputations are usually earned."

"Then I'm even more surprised by the subject matter." Paloma raised an eyebrow at him. "The paintings are all of women, yes, but these women are not objects in these paintings. They're individuals."

"And my husband wouldn't have chosen images of women as individuals?"

Paul shrugged. "I've never even met the man," he said, "but if his reputation is earned, as you say, then I would think he'd choose works with a more traditional representation of women."

"Ones that objectify them?"

"Yes. Is your husband a collector?"

"Of women?"

"Of art."

Paloma chuckled without humor. "He collects money," she said, "and things that will impress other people."

"If his goal were to impress visitors, he would have chosen works from artists more famous and recognizable than these. And if he wanted a reflection of his own view toward women, those artists would have given him plenty of choices. But these paintings," he pointed at the artwork on the wall, "don't serve either of those purposes."

"You seem to know a lot about art, Mr. Baker."

Paul put his hands in his pockets and shrugged. "Not really. I'm just a dabbler."

"Are you an artist?"

"I'm an investor," Paul smiled.

Paloma arched her eyebrows and appraised Paul for a moment. His heart skipped two beats in his chest as she did.

"Are you a collector?"

"Of art?"

Paloma shrugged one shoulder. Her hair slipped from it, revealing smooth skin and a thin dress strap that caressed the curve of her shoulder. "Of anything."

Paul gulped again. "No," he said. His mouth was suddenly parched, his voice hoarse. He cleared his throat. "No, not really."

"Do you enjoy reading?" she asked as she led him into the library.

"I do," said Paul, "though I don't have as much time for it as I'd like."

"No one ever does," said Paloma. She walked through the room, up to a bookshelf against the far wall, and pressed both hands against it. "But if you want something in your life," she looked over her shoulder at him, "you have to make time for it."

The shelf swiveled open, revealing a salon beyond. Paloma smiled at the surprise that must have shown on Paul's face, then stepped through the secret door. Paul followed, watching as the door swung shut behind him. Just like the crew entry to the wheelhouse stairs, from where he stood inside the salon, the door appeared to be a seamless part of the wall. It even had a light switch on it. He flicked the switch up and down and a light above him turned on and off.

The salon was massive, with a large semicircular couch in front of a flat-screen television in one section, a large dining table surrounded by eight chairs in another, and several smaller sets of tables and chairs in another section. As in the rest of the yacht, the appointments were luxurious and expensive. Unlike the rest of the yacht, in this room they were also tasteful, blending into a coherent whole that was anything but chaotic. Paul found himself relaxing just by stepping into the elegant space.

The entire wall opposite Paul opened to a deck. He could see cleverly disguised tracks in the ceiling where the wall could be closed to insulate the salon from inclement weather. But tonight it was wide open. He could hear the chatter of the guests on the decks below. The glow of the deck lights complemented the soft lighting of the salon, giving the entire space the sense of one unending flow from interior to exterior.

"Would you like something to drink?" asked Paloma, stepping behind a bar.

"No, thank you," said Paul.

"You don't drink?"

"I do, but there's no need for you to serve me. I'm sure I can find a drink elsewhere."

"And what if I want to serve you?" said Paloma. "Am I allowed to do that?"

Paul frowned. "Why would you want to serve me?"

Paloma pushed out her bottom lip and tilted her head from side to side. "You haven't tried to impress me with your money. You haven't tried to bully me into the bedroom. You seem to actually listen when I speak. You seem like a decent man. That's enough to earn you a drink."

"Seems like a pretty low bar."

"And yet, so few men are able to clear it." She held up a bottle. "Whiskey?"

Paul smiled. "Sounds great."

He stood at the border between the inside of the salon and the deck. The deck was a good twenty feet deep, at least, but he didn't want to be seen by the crowd downstairs. He was trying to attract as little attention as possible, and being seen alone with

Paloma Minsk on the deck of her private salon would definitely defeat that purpose.

Paloma came up beside him with two tumblers, each with two fingers of whiskey in it. She gave one to Paul, clinked her glass against his, held it up in a silent toast, and took a long sip. Paul did the same. The whiskey was smooth and complex. A riot of flavors spilled over his tongue. Soil and smoke and spice and sweetness. There was no burn to the whiskey at all, either on Paul's tongue or in his throat when he swallowed. It was, hands down, the finest whiskey he'd ever tasted.

"I don't blame you for standing back here," Paloma said, tilting her head toward him conspiratorially. "And I don't blame you for sneaking around the ship. I would do the same if I were you. These kinds of parties are a chore. So many people who already have so much, all still looking for more."

"Why do you suppose that is?"

Paloma looked at him, surprise on her face. "Don't you know?"

Paul couldn't imagine what she meant by that question. He shook his head, perplexed.

"What they lack can't be replaced by money or the things money can buy. And the holes inside them can't be filled by the favor of other empty people. But they don't know that, so they keep trying to fill themselves, over and over. The more they earn, the more they consume. The more they consume, the emptier they feel. They're in hell, but they think they're in paradise. And that makes their hell all the more painful for them."

Paul listened to the chatter of guests outside, imagined their tuxedos and jewels and high heels and expensive watches. And he imagined the boredom on their faces, the weariness in their manner. "What is it they lack, then?"

Paloma tilted her head at him.

"Self-respect," she said, "of course."

8

ONE OF THE doors to Paloma's salon slid open behind them. Paul and Paloma turned at the same time to see the man in the tuxedo walking toward them. It was the same man Paul had seen in the office earlier, the one that had been walking upstairs when he crept from the art gallery. He still carried his silver laptop under one arm.

"All in order, Vern?" said Paloma.

"Yes, Mrs. Minsk," said the man. "All in order."

The man was tall, thin, and impeccably dressed, with his cuffs extending exactly one inch from his tuxedo jacket on both arms, his bow tie perfectly straight and balanced, his shoes polished to a gleam. What hair he still had was neatly trimmed and combed, and his bald pate was as shiny as his shoes. Even his silver-rimmed glasses seemed to be spotless in the light drifting from the ceiling of the salon.

"Vernon Stratham, this is Mr. Paul Baker, one of our guests for the evening."

"A pleasure to meet you, Mr. Baker. I hope you're enjoying the party."

"No one enjoys these parties, Vern," said Paloma with a venomous smile.

Vernon pressed his lips together in what to him must have passed for a smile.

"Nice to meet you, too, Mr. Stratham," said Paul, shaking Vernon's hand. Vernon's grip was firm, his handshake quick. His pressed-lip smile did not extend to his eyes. Paul got the sense that this was a man who would rather be back in the office working than out here meeting someone new.

"Vern works with Attorney General Jenkins. His... what do you call it, Vern? His bean counter? Mathmagician?"

"Campaign finance chairperson," said Vernon with a curt nod.

"Campaign finance chairperson," said Paloma, saying the words with a silky purr. "Such a seductive title." She took a sip from her drink. "Vern and my husband are old friends."

"Not friends," said Vernon to Paul. "Mr. Minsk has been a staunch and loyal supporter of the Attorney General for years."

"That means he gives him a lot of money," said Paloma to Paul.

"He's a very generous man," nodded Vernon. "As such, he and I have had reason to work together often."

"Vern launders my husband's money for him. Some of it, anyway."

Vernon stared at his shoes for a long moment. "I believe your husband may be misunderstood. Reputations often don't reflect reality, especially for public figures like Mr. Minsk."

"And the Attorney General?" said Paloma.

"No public figure is immune to rumor."

Paloma snorted into her glass as she took another drink. Her demeanor had changed completely since Vernon had entered the room. Where before she had been thoughtful and compassionate, she had become almost petulant. It was clear she found Vernon to be unsettling, but Paul couldn't see why. The man was a stuffed suit, for sure, about as joyful as unexploded ordinance, but that didn't make him a bad person.

And the fact that he worked for AG Jenkins instantly made him Paul's Plan B. He eyed Vernon's laptop. Maybe even Plan A.

No, Paul would stick with the original plan until it fell apart. That's what his parents had always taught him, and that's what he would do. For all he knew, Vernon's laptop had nothing but Solitaire and Minesweeper high scores on it.

"You can see that Vern is quite the politician, Paul," said Paloma. "I'm sure he would run for office himself, if he could." She turned and smiled sweetly at Vernon. "But people need to like a candidate before they'll vote for them. That disqualifies Vern."

Vernon nodded toward his shoes again, then cast a quick, almost apologetic glance up at Paul. "Fortunately for me," he said, "my work stays behind the scenes. Yours, however, does not, Mrs. Minsk." He held one hand out toward the deck. "I believe it's time for you to begin the event."

"What about Devin?" said Paloma. "They're all here for him, anyway. Let him start things off."

"He asked me to have you greet the crowd first, Mrs. Minsk."

Paloma blew a raspberry. "Typical. Make me do his dirty work." She tossed back the rest of her drink and set the glass on a table with a thunk. "You'll have to excuse me, Mr. Baker," she said. "I have to sing for my supper now."

She strode onto the deck. Vernon gave Paul another apologetic glance, then followed Paloma.

When Paloma reached the rail, her entire demeanor changed. Even from behind, her body language grew more expansive, more energetic. A natural performer. She spread her arms wide and called out to the crowd. "Welcome, my dear friends, and thank you all for coming tonight."

As the crowd clapped politely, Vernon took up station to one side of the deck, hidden in the shadows, watching Paloma and the crowd. Paul finished his whiskey, savoring one last delicious sip, then took the opportunity to slip out the door unseen.

The sound of Paloma's voice cut off when the door to the salon slid shut behind Paul. The lobby was quiet and still. All he could hear now was the silence of the stairwell and the faint, distant hum of the yacht itself. All of the guests would be occupied with Paloma's speech. The crew would be occupied with serving the guests or piloting the yacht. Now was the perfect time for Paul to slip upstairs to the owner's suite and find what he came for.

There was only one loose end, of course.

The owner.

Paul still hadn't spotted Minsk. And if he wasn't outside with Paloma, greeting the guests and getting the campaign donations started, he must still be upstairs getting ready.

But Paul couldn't wait any longer. This was too perfect an opportunity to get upstairs unseen. And if the owner's suite was half as elaborate as the deck he had been on with Paloma, there'd be plenty of places for Paul to hide.

Or so he hoped.

9

Paul crept up the central staircase slowly, deliberately. He took one step, gently setting his foot down and pressing himself up, then waited, listening, watching as best he could around the curve of the stair. He heard nothing. He saw nothing. Just the soft, distant hum of the ship's machinery and the hissing silence of the air conditioning piped into the space.

When he got to the top, he was relieved to find that the staircase didn't open into the middle of a giant lounge or lobby like it had on the decks below. Instead, on this deck it opened to a vestibule with walls close on all sides and covered in beautiful paintings of seascapes, all blues and greens and sea-foam whites. The passageway in front of him was carpeted in thick pile, and narrow enough for Paul to touch the other side if he reached out his arm.

Without immediate risk of being seen, Paul had a moment to gather himself, to listen and get his bearings before he turned the corner into a room where he could be spotted. Again, he heard nothing at all. Just machinery and air. Was Minsk still up there? Had he already used some other stairwell to go downstairs to greet his guests?

Paul thought back to the deck plans he'd memorized. Every

yacht varied somewhat from the general plans developed by the builder, and Paul had already encountered a number of customizations during his tour. A wall removed here, another erected there. A room that was a galley in the plans was now part of a salon. Real changes, but nothing so major that the plans were no longer useful.

The plan for the owner's deck included a lounge on one side that opened to a small patio with a hot tub jutting out from the very top level of the ship, overlooking the sea and the decks below. That was toward the bow of the ship. Paul oriented himself mentally, difficult after the twisting staircase, and decided that the bow of the ship was to his left.

According to Paul's mental map, toward the stern of the ship on Paul's right there should be a small office on the left side of the passageway. The passageway would then open into the owner's bedroom suite, with a dressing area immediately to the left, a bathroom across from it on the right, and the bedroom straight ahead. Beyond that, the bedroom opened onto another weather deck, directly above the deck where Paloma was standing and speaking at that moment.

There were stairs connecting each of the weather decks. Since Paul could hear only dead quiet all around him, Minsk may have already gone down to join Paloma. If so, Paul had a window of opportunity. He needed to get into that office.

He took a deep, slow breath, screwed up his courage, then let the breath out as he stepped into the passageway, relaxing his muscles so as to move quickly and quietly. Tension was the enemy of any job, and Paul had to regulate his own breathing to eliminate as much tension from his body as he possibly could.

He darted around the corner to his right, kept both his body and his eyes moving, his ears open. He saw no one, heard nothing. He pulled his breath in through his nose in a long, slow draught, released it slowly, silently through his mouth. Long, quiet, calming breaths, just as his parents had taught him.

He found the office, slid inside with a minimum of movement, opening the door just wide enough for his body, then closing it tightly behind him. There was a single window that looked onto the passageway. His back against the door, Paul peered through from the side, watching for any movement, any sign that he'd been spotted. None came.

The window had a curtain. Paul snapped it shut so he couldn't be seen. He locked the office door. If someone tried to enter, the locked door would probably be unusual and might set off alarm bells. But there was only one door to the office, and Paul wanted some advance notice—even just a few seconds—if he was going to be spotted.

The wall opposite the door was lined with windows, offering Paul a beautiful view of the dark bay, the sliver of moon in the sky, and the shoreline, now tiny in the distance. They must be near the outside of the bay, closest to the open ocean. Paul couldn't see the lights of the other ships at all, and the lights of the buildings on shore had been reduced to a narrow band, an artificial horizon.

Paloma was right. It was a long way for a getaway. But Paul didn't intend for his theft to be detected. If he could pull it off, there would be no getaway needed.

The office had an L-shaped desk attached to the wall below the windows. A couch lay along one bulkhead, a wet bar and cabinet along another. Two cushy, swiveling armchairs hunched between the couch and the desk.

Most importantly to Paul, a computer monitor sat on the desk. No laptop here, just a monitor. Minsk didn't seem the type to carry his work around with him. He had minions for that. But he was known to keep meticulous records of his dealings, both the legitimate ones and the illegitimate ones, and to check them regularly. He was an oaf and a thug, but he was also a smart businessman. Smart businessmen knew to keep track of their numbers.

Paul slipped into the chair behind the desk and found a keyboard and mouse on a sliding tray underneath. He turned on the monitor and woke the computer. It immediately opened to the desktop screen.

Minsk was a smart businessman, but he was shit for IT. Paul had spent a long evening at a bar with a former employee of a firm Minsk had once used for compliance work. The evening had been dull, and Paul's hangover had been cruel, but he'd gotten the information he was hoping for.

The employee had told him that Minsk was notoriously unable to remember a password, and didn't have the patience for biometrics, which were often glitchy and cumbersome. He never locked his phone or his computers. His idea of information security took the form of armed staff and a reputation filled with stories of a ruthless and bloody past.

Minsk hired people to make sure all of his data was backed up in a thousand places so it would never be lost, and to make sure that any compromised device could be remotely wiped, tracked, and destroyed, if necessary. It was laughable, really, for a man as wealthy and criminal as Minsk. Ridiculously lax. But, Minsk was a ridiculous man. And the wealthy always seemed to think themselves invincible. Supermen on helipads.

And now Paul was using that arrogance to his advantage.

He opened a terminal window on the computer and ran a system-wide search for files that would contain financial information. Database files, spreadsheets, CSV files. Anything that might contain the records of Minsk's dealings.

The computer returned a long slew of filenames. Paul scanned through them quickly, looking for patterns in the naming conventions. Logical, technical people, like computer programmers, accountants, finance people, and the like, typically used logical names for their files. While your average retired gentleman might call his financial tracking spreadsheet "Tom's Investment Tracker.xlsx", a professional who created those kinds of files all the time and was likely to have to find them quickly, on demand, was more likely to name it something like "MinskShipping_AccountsReceivable_2023Q1.csv".

That was Paul's hope, anyway. But there were so many files that Paul could tell right away he would get nowhere with that approach. There were too many for him to scan through manually. He added some commands to filter the results further, looking for filenames with various keywords in them. Minsk's name, the names of Minsk's companies, financial accounting terms like "accounts receivable" or "tax deductions", even "charitable donations". That cut down the list, but still returned hundreds of files.

Paul modified the search commands to search the text of the files themselves instead of just the filenames, then added a parameter to include the name "Jenkins". It was a long shot. If the Attorney General was taking illicit funds from Minsk, he would probably be smart enough to hide the paper trail behind a pseudonym, and probably behind a series of shell companies, too.

But this wasn't the Attorney General's computer. This was Minsk's computer, and anyone dumb enough to work without passwords was dumb enough—or arrogant enough—to work without pseudonyms. For all Paul knew, if Minsk had so much trouble remembering passwords, he might have trouble remembering the pseudonyms for all the politicians and government employees he was bribing around the world.

Paul finished entering the command and hit the return key on the keyboard. This was a far more taxing search. The computer had to look through the contents of each one of the thousands of files, looking for the keywords Paul had specified. That meant more relevant results, hopefully, but it also meant more time for each search. And time was something Paul might not have.

His knee bounced under the desk while he watched the progress bar on the computer inch to the right as the computer worked. Paul forced himself to push back from the desk, to stand and walk to the door. He focused on his breathing again, long, deep breaths, calming himself. He pushed the computer search from his mind and opened his senses instead. Peering out the sides of the curtain over the window, he checked the passageway again. Still no one there. He listened carefully. Again, all he could hear was the machinery and the hermetic silence of the air conditioning. Paul shivered, suddenly cold. The AC must really have been cranked up.

Killing time, he looked around the room more carefully than he had before, looking for signs of recent use. He found nothing. The chair cushions were undented. The couch cushions were practically brand new. He opened the cabinet above the bar. All of the bottles were neatly ordered. A small serving tray was tucked into a special slot in the side of the cupboard. A variety of glasses—champagne flutes, brandy snifters, beer and wine glasses, and so on—were all sparkling clean, aligned in neat rows. Two were missing from a row of tumblers with an unusual off-kilter octagonal cut, and one tall bottle was turned with the back facing out, but nothing else seemed to have been disturbed. Aside from that bottle, the seals on the others hadn't even been broken.

Paul turned the bottle until the label faced front again. Beluga Vodka, from Russia. *Impressively pure and smooth, with notes of vanilla, sage, white pepper, and cream,* according to the label copy. Figured. Minsk was a notorious lush. Paul was surprised that the bar had anything left in it at all.

His nerves finally calmed once again, Paul checked the computer. The progress bar was at one hundred percent. The search was complete.

But it had returned nothing.

No files in the system containing the name "Jenkins".

He ran another search, looking for any combination of the terms "Attorney General" or "AG". He added misspellings like

"Jenkin", or "Jenkens". Paul threw in every term he could think of that might return a useful match. While he waited for the computer to ponder these modifications, his knee bounced madly under the desk. Paul didn't bother trying to stop it, just stared at the damn black-and-white progress bar inching along the screen, willing it to move faster, willing it to return something he could use.

It returned nothing.

Paul wanted to scream. He wanted to throw the monitor across the room, to smash it into a hundred pieces against the wall. He wanted to drink five fingers of whatever booze was strongest in that bar, then use the bottle to smash everything in the room.

He let himself think those thoughts, feel that frustration for thirty seconds. Then he pulled himself back into the present moment again.

This was Plan A.

Plan A was not working.

Time for Plan B.

Quickly, Paul checked the computer to see where the data was coming from, where the files were stored, and how much space they took up. As he expected, the data was all stored in the cloud, taking up way more storage than he could copy onto a thumb drive, or even onto a laptop. There was no way he was going to steal Minsk's entire filesystem and comb through it later.

Maybe he could copy the locations and figure out how to access them from his own home? That was unlikely. Minsk may be an idiot with a capital I and a capital T, but the people who maintained his servers wouldn't be. They would have layers of security on the data, and they would have sniffers to watch carefully where the data was accessed from. If the data were accessed from anywhere unusual, anywhere that Minsk wasn't, they would likely be alerted. Paul was good with computers, but he was no cybersecurity expert.

He felt a pang in his heart at the thought. He wasn't a cybersecurity expert, but he knew one. She would be able to crack Minsk's data without breaking a sweat. Paul had no doubt about that.

He pushed the thought from his mind. It wasn't an option.

Plan A was failing. Plan B was a no go, too. What was Plan C?

Minsk had dealings with thousands of people. Trying to find a few entries in the sea of data that represented his transactions was too much. Paul had misjudged the opportunity. He thought if he could get onto the yacht and access Minsk's computer system, he could find the data he needed. And maybe he still could. He took a thumb drive from his pocket and copied all the files from his last productive search. A couple hundred files, more or less randomly copied. Maybe they would yield something useful, maybe not.

It was a lame, scattershot, desperate plan. Plans dependent on luck were not plans, they were prayers. Paul had to find more reliable information.

Paul slipped the thumb drive into his jacket pocket, then smiled as a thought came to him. He had to know more about Minsk's dealings with AG Jenkins. Who better to provide that information than Jenkins' campaign finance chairperson himself, Paul's newest friend, Vernon Stratham?

10

PAUL PEERED through the curtains to be certain the passageway was empty in both directions. Seeing no one, he slid out of the office and gentled the door shut behind him. Before finding Stratham amid the dull babel of the guests below, it was worth checking the rest of the deck. Maybe Minsk had another computer or a phone or laptop that would prove more useful than the last one.

Paul crept along the passageway toward the master bedroom. He passed the dressing room, saw shelves filled with leather shoes in wild designs, including several with long, tapered toes that looked almost like something Santa's elves would wear. Some were made of skins that looked like they came from endangered animals, others that were more like sneakers that looked like they were made from recycled marshmallows. And gold, gold, gold. Everywhere was gold. From the shoes to the rows of jackets to the shirts and pants. Minsk even had a section of his dressing area dedicated to a dozen pairs of golden jeans. Sigmund Freud would have lost his mind in that room.

In the center was an island, a block with shelves on both

sides and racks on the top. The shelves were likely filled with socks and underwear—if Minsk even wore underwear—but the racks were filled with watches and jewelry. It felt like a cross between a high-end jeweler in New York City and a pawn shop in Compton. (Ironically, both locations were likely to have an armed security guard stationed out front.) Minsk's style of dress was as decadent as his style in everything else. Money, money, money. Show, show, show.

Opposite the dressing room, Paul glanced in at the bathroom. Huge and ornate, it had a pass-through design. He could see all the way through the open far door to a passageway on the opposite side.

Gaudy gold was everywhere in the bathroom, too. Gold faucets and handles. Gold mirrors. Gold sconces. Gold trim on the shower. Even flecks of gold in the white tile on the walls and floor. Paul wondered idly if the fixtures were made of solid gold or just gold plated. He decided solid gold was more likely. It was more expensive and far more impractical, which made it the obvious choice for someone like Minsk.

Neither the dressing room nor the bathroom were occupied. Paul couldn't see anything or hear anything as he crept along, controlling his breathing. But he did detect a smell, growing stronger. Where the scent on Paloma's deck had been floral and sweet, this one was acrid and pungent.

Cigar smoke.

Active cigar smoke. It didn't have the stale smell of decay, like an old man waiting to die, that comes from a cigar that had been extinguished some time ago. This scent was angry and combative. The cigar was still lit. And the smell was coming from the bedroom, directly ahead.

Paul crept closer, shallowing his breathing so he wouldn't cough from the smell, but keeping the rhythm of his breaths regular. He moved slow, with loose, relaxed muscles. Tension made noise. Tension caused mistakes. The most important thing in any job was to keep your mind and your body as relaxed as possible.

The soft carpet of the passageway had turned to tile outside the bathroom. Paul placed each shoe slowly, deliberately, then pressed his weight into the balls of his feet and leaned forward, his ear beside the corner of the bedroom bulkhead, listening, extending his senses to feel the room, to feel for any energy there that might represent another person.

Nothing.

The scent of the cigar was stronger. It had to be in the bedroom, burning. But Paul couldn't hear or feel anything else. Maybe Minsk had gone below and left his cigar burning in an ashtray. Maybe, as Paul had thought earlier, Minsk had joined Paloma in greeting the crowd.

That meant he could be back soon. Paul had to get moving. He pulled in a silent breath. As he released it, he poked his head around the corner, into the bedroom.

No one was there. Across the room, on a table in the far corner, a cigar burned in an ashtray, thick white smoke curling up toward the ceiling before being whisked away by a very robust ventilation system.

The bedroom was large, but, surprisingly, not excessive. Beside Paul, against the bulkhead shared with the bathroom, sat a king-size bed, neatly made. Gold satin pillows fluffed and arranged at the head atop a shiny gold comforter and what looked like gold silk sheets. Paul nearly vomited at the thought of Minsk rolling around in those sheets.

A large television hung on the wall to the left and the table with the cigar sat to the right, two chairs arranged around it. At the end of the bed, a set of sliding doors opened to a small deck. Paul walked to the foot of the bed, triggering the sliding doors to open. He stepped through.

The deck had a long couch and several smaller chairs arranged around a table with a gas firepit in the center, the flames burning away. The light from the flames and from the lights set into the side rails was low and warm and as golden as the decor. Triangular sails stretched overhead. They would serve to keep the sun off of the guests during the day, but at night, they blacked out the stars and loomed overhead like the wings of giant bats.

On Paul's right, a curling staircase went up to the helicopter pad above. On his left, stairs descended to the deck below. Paul could hear Paloma's voice from down there, could hear laughter and clapping as the guests responded to some comment she made. Paloma was an entertainer, a professional. Whether she'd come to that skill naturally or had been forced to learn it since she'd married Minsk, Paul didn't know. But for someone who claimed to hate this kind of party, she seemed to have the crowd in the palm of her hand.

The rail of the balcony was made of glass. Paul crept closer, trying to get a look at the crowd, trying to peek at the deck below to see if Minsk had joined Paloma. Paul stayed to the side of the deck, in the shadows. As he inched forward, he could see the faces of the guests through the rail, all eyes fixed on Paloma. The sequins of the ladies' dresses winked in the light. The men's cuff links sparked like stars. The crystal in the glasses of champagne they held refracted the light into tiny sprays of color. Paul crept closer, close enough to see the back of Paloma's head.

She stood at the rail on the deck below Paul. Alone. Minsk was not beside her.

If he wasn't beside her, where was he?

Paul ducked back into the bedroom and made his way past the smoking cigar. It rested in a crystal ashtray, grey smoke curling up, a withered inch-long finger of ash at its tip. Whoever owned this cigar hadn't smoked it in a while.

Paul moved on, down the opposite side of the bed from

where he'd come in. The other passageway ran ahead of him, down the length of the deck on the starboard side of the ship. Paul moved quickly, silently. He passed the door to the bathroom, now on his right. Windows lined the wall to his left.

Up ahead, Paul could see brighter light. He remembered the deck plans. The passageway would open to an owner's lounge at the bow end of the ship. He slowed as he neared the opening, crept forward and peered around the corner.

A couch and several chairs were arranged in the room. Two tables in the corners. A small bar set in one wall. A large skylight overhead, refracting the dim moonlight through prismed panes of glass.

No one was in that room, either.

On the far wall was another sliding glass door. From the deck plans, Paul knew it would open to yet another outdoor deck, this one semi-circular in shape, much smaller than the deck extending off of the bedroom.

He could see it faintly through the dark glass, the inset lighting outside making everything look like a shadow. Paul could make out the seating that ringed the rail, with short stairs in the center that led to a hot tub that overlooked the bow of the ship. The throne of the king.

Paul stepped up to the door. It slid open with a soft hiss. The deck was cozy. The hot tub was made of glass. Three teak stairs rose to its rim, leaving the pale blue-green water visible between the treads. Lit from underwater lights, it bubbled and steamed, murmuring softly in the moonlight, a Greek chorus above the sound of the low waves cut by the bow of the ship well below.

Soft, white-cushioned seats arced along the rail on either side of the hot tub, golden lights along their base adding to the soft glow from the water. It was a beautiful, peaceful place. The colors, the sounds, the breeze from the movement of the ship blowing through the steam of the hot tub, warming it slightly before it kissed Paul's cheeks. If Paul were the owner, he would spend a lot of time on that deck.

But he was not the owner. And there were no computers there, no phones or laptops. Nothing of use to Paul. With one last look to drink in the beautiful scene, he turned to leave.

And saw Devin Minsk sitting in the corner.

11

PAUL'S HEART rate went from a peaceful tap to a frantic hammer in the blink of an eye. Only sheer willpower and a childhood of training allowed him to focus on his breathing and control his sudden anxiety.

Most people, when frightened, close down. They get tunnel vision and focus only on what is in front of them. It helps them to ignore extraneous detail and escape a dangerous situation. But in situations like this, it was more helpful to pull in as much information as possible. Extraneous details often held the key to a clever—or just plain lucky—escape.

Paul controlled his breathing and opened his senses. The lights became sharper, the colors more saturated. He felt the cool slap of the wind against his cheeks and the back of his neck. He smelled alcohol and lingering cigar smoke and sea salt and chlorine, could taste them on his tongue, still thick from the whiskey he'd drunk with Paloma. The sound of the waves, the murmuring hot tub, the creak of the ship, the hum of the machinery, the laughter of the guests, all of this sensory input swirled in Paul's mind like paint mixing on an artist's palette, mixing with the sight directly in front of him.

Minsk sat in the shadows on a cushion in the corner where

65

the curve of the small deck met the corner of the bulkhead. Hidden in the semi-darkness, Paul couldn't see his face, but Minsk's body was rigid and upright. He sat like a man in a conference room during a tense business negotiation, his knees bent at a perfect right angle, the stripe of his tuxedo pants like a carpenter's square.

In his hand was a tumbler, one from his office with the unusual off-kilter octagonal cut. Condensation stood like goose-bumps on the side, dripping like tearfalls down the glass and over his hand. His skin was pallid in the ethereal light from the hot tub, his white cuffs stark against his tuxedo jacket, practically glowing in the shadows. In the glass, ice cubes melted into two fingers of a clear liquid. Probably vodka, given Minsk's Russian heritage.

Even though Paul wasn't supposed to be there, had barged in without warning or preamble, Minsk didn't move, didn't speak, didn't acknowledge Paul in any way. That set Paul's warning bells to ringing.

"I'm so sorry," he stammered, immediately playing the role of the caught-out party snooper like he had with Paloma earlier. "I didn't mean to disturb you." He put on his most charming smile. "Your yacht is so beautiful, I couldn't resist exploring."

Minsk didn't reply. Didn't move. Didn't react at all. Didn't even take a swig of his drink. If Paul had been on his own private deck, enjoying a quiet moment in the midst of a party, he wouldn't sit impassively while a guest crashed in on the scene. He'd play the generous host and invite the visitor to sit with him, or he'd get angry or annoyed and yell at him to leave. Or he'd escort the intruder back to the party and subtly encourage him to mind his own business for the rest of the night. Whatever it was, he'd do *something*.

From Minsk's reputation, Paul would have put his money on anger and annoyance. He certainly wouldn't have guessed that

Minsk would sit completely immobile while Paul babbled apologies.

Something was up.

Paul wished he could shine the light of his phone in Minsk's face, could see what Minsk was doing. He switched from feigned apology to feigned concern. "Mr. Minsk?" he said, one arm outstretched in a helpful gesture, stepping closer and trying to see Minsk's face in the shadows, "are you alright?"

Minsk still didn't respond. Paul's concern became real, not for Minsk, but for himself. Something was definitely not right here. The Greek chorus in the hot tub was pointing and chanting a warning at high volume. Paul moved closer, close enough now to finally make out some detail in the darkness.

He could see one side of Minsk's face. Minsk's expression was utterly impassive. Eyes open and unblinking, he stared straight ahead as if in a daze. Maybe he'd taken a hit of something, some drug that had left him immobile? Heroin or ketamine, maybe? Minsk didn't have a reputation as a drug addict. Alcoholic, for sure, but not a drug user. But maybe he'd tried something that night. Or maybe someone had dosed him.

Paul crept even closer, reaching out his hand. He was close enough to touch Minsk now, his hand hovering near Minsk's forearm where it rested on his thigh. Paul wouldn't touch him, of course. He didn't want to intrude, didn't want to leave a mark. But this all felt too off, too weird.

The wind gusted. The hot tub burbled and spit. Paul felt drops of hot water blown against his cheek, burning like pinprick embers in the increasingly cool night.

They burned like a warning bell clanging. It was time for Paul to leave. Now.

Minsk moved, fast. Too fast for Paul to react. In one blink, Minsk was catatonic. In the next, he had Paul's wrist in a vice. Minsk stood, his grip crushing, bending Paul's hand and wrist backwards. Pain speared up Paul's arm into his elbow, then his shoulder.

Minsk's other arm fell to his side, spilling his drink across the wood floor with a thin splat and a skitter of ice. As he forced Paul backward, Minsk's eyes came into the light first, wide and wild and filled with panic. Dark eyes that reflected Paul's face, screwed in pain, his own eyes just as wide as Minsk's.

Minsk kept moving forward, kept pushing Paul backward. Finally, like a door opening, the light spread full across Minsk's face, bringing it into clear view.

Paul gasped out loud.

A deep gash cut across the left side of Minsk's forehead and into his hairline. Blood oozed over his left eye, across his temple, and down his cheek. His hair on that side was soaked and matted.

Minsk twisted Paul's wrist further. Paul curled his body with the motion, trying to relieve the stabs of white-hot pain arcing through his arm. He felt like his shoulder would twist from its socket. Paul was not a tiny man, but Minsk had at least a hundred pounds on him, maybe one-fifty. And he moved with the force and focus of a man untethered, a man who had spent many years torturing and killing people who got in his way.

Paul's gorge rose in his throat. With it came desperation. He balled his free hand into a fist and chopped it down on Minsk's forearm, trying to get him to let go. It was like punching a dead man. Minsk didn't even flinch.

As he twisted further, as Paul cried out, Minsk's expression never wavered. Still that same wild-eyed impassivity, as blank-faced and menacing as a horror show slasher.

Paul's pain became more desperate, his reactions more primal. If he didn't get Minsk to let go, Paul would wind up with a broken arm or a dislocated shoulder. Or worse. He stopped chopping on Minsk's forearm and swung at Minsk's face instead. He landed one punch solid against Minsk's jaw, pain now spearing up both of Paul's arms. Minsk's head snapped to the side as the punch landed, but his grip never loosened, his inexorable forward push never slowed. When his face came back around to the front, it bore the same wild-eyed blankness it had a moment ago.

A childhood of training or not, Paul's anxiety spiked then. He lost all sense of propriety or strategy. He hacked away at Minsk's forearm, bringing his fist down again and again, his preservation instinct trying anything to free him from that grip. When beating Minsk's forearm didn't work, Paul backhanded Minsk's chin. When that had no effect, he set his feet and punched Minsk in the chest, stepping into Minsk's forward movement to deliver the blow.

Minsk stopped dead, like Paul had punched an off switch. He dropped Paul's arm. Paul stumbled backward, crumpled onto the soft seats along the rail. The pain in his arm still seared, but thankfully was already receding. No permanent damage done.

Minsk dropped the empty tumbler he still held in his left hand. It fell to the wood floor and rolled away in a low, scraping drumroll, then wobbled back and forth before settling. Minsk looked down at his chest, at the place Paul had punched him. He brought his hand up under his tuxedo coat, pulled it back.

Covered in blood.

Minsk pulled open his jacket. The side of his white shirt was red and soaked, clinging to the bulbous shape of Minsk's gut.

Paul hadn't noticed it before, focused on freeing his arm. But he couldn't miss the blood now. He looked down at his own hand, formed the fist he'd used to punch Minsk. Paul's knuckles were red and slick. He fought the sudden urge to wipe them clean on the white seat cushions. Didn't want to leave a mark. Didn't want to raise questions.

When he looked up again, Minsk was climbing the steps to the hot tub, slow and steady and impassive as an automaton. He reached the top step. Without hesitation, he stepped again, splashing down into the hot tub with first one leg, then the other, then back up the other side.

He balanced there on a small strip of wood between the hot tub and the low glass rail that surrounded the small deck. Water sluiced down his legs, pooled at his feet. Minsk didn't seem to care, didn't even seem to notice.

"Minsk," said Paul, rising to his feet, standing beside the stairs. His pulse pounded in his ears. "Minsk, come down."

Minsk turned his head, staring over his shoulder at Paul. His eyes were no longer wild.

Now they were as expressionless as his face.

Just like that, head turned, expression blank, dead eyes locked on Paul's, Devin Minsk tipped over the side of the low rail and fell.

12

THE WIND CARRIED to Paul's ears the tharumping sound of Minsk's body hitting the deck below, then carried it away again, leaving behind the murmur of the bubbling hot tub, the cut of the ship's bow in the low waves. A thin peal of laughter somehow fought through the wind from the crowd at the back of the ship.

Paul scrambled to the rail, looked over the side at Minsk's body. One arm was pinned under Minsk's chest, the other flung out to the side, the legs in an unnatural tangle. The neck was twisted so that, though his chest rested on the deck below, Minsk's eyes, now truly dead, still stared up at Paul. They seemed to stare right into him, into his soul, to see straight through him to who he really was.

And Paul couldn't look away. Much as he wanted to, he couldn't look away. His mind replayed the scene from a few moments earlier. The manic power that Minsk had used to twist Paul's arm. The wildness in his eyes. The way he'd marched, like a robot, through the hot tub and over the rail, all wildness gone, replaced with slow, inevitable death, even before he fell.

Only Minsk hadn't died. He'd been murdered.

The gash on his head could have been accidental. A bad fall

71

in the shower, or too much vodka and a sudden lurch when the ship hit a rogue wave.

But the blood on Minsk's shirt was from a knife to the heart, or a gunshot, or something. He had been dying, there on the seat in the shadows in the corner. It was a miracle he hadn't died already. He must have used the last of his strength to attack Paul, some last gasp of otherworldly strength before he accepted his fate and stepped to his death.

Paul stared over the rail at the body, the scene replaying over and over in his mind.

Then the captain was there, and the blonde woman, the first officer. They looked at Minsk's crumpled body, then up at Paul. Paul broke his gaze from Minsk's dead eyes, slid them to the captain's stern ones. Without looking away from Paul, the captain spat on Minsk's body, turned, and strode purposefully back into the wheelhouse.

A stab of panic ran up Paul's spine as his thoughts turned away from Minsk's predicament and toward his own. Minsk was dead, fallen from the upper deck, and the captain and his first officer had seen Paul there.

He pushed back from the rail, looked down at his hand, still slick with blood. Minsk's blood.

Not good.

Paul stabbed his fist into the hot tub. It burned. He watched the red blood lift into claw-like strands, like a demon releasing its grip on Paul's fist, then dissolve in the pale blue-green water. Paul shook his hand under the water, then pulled it out and scrubbed it with his other hand. There was no blood visible on his fist anymore, but Paul scrubbed it anyway, then dunked it back in the water to rinse.

He forced himself to focus, tore his mind from what he'd just witnessed and forced himself to focus on the present moment. He'd witnessed a death, most likely a murder. Or at least a homicide. And worse, his witnessing had itself been witnessed.

Paul had been seen at the scene of a crime.

He had to disappear.

There would be no evidence of his presence, nothing that would tie him to the death. A few eyewitness accounts of Paul Baker, a man who didn't exist. No fingerprints. No forensic evidence that wouldn't mingle with the evidence of a hundred other guests, indistinguishable. Nothing that would lead police definitively to Paul's doorstep.

But still, Paul had to leave. Minsk's death was hardly a tragedy. The world would be a better place. But it was definitely newsworthy. And Paul needed to make sure the news had no trace of him in it.

He would have liked to leave the party altogether, but one glance over the rail told Paul that would be difficult. The lights of the shoreline were distant stars along the horizon.

Besides, Paul still hadn't gotten what he came for. He needed to get back to the party, blend in with the guests until he could formulate a new plan, a plan that would get him the data he needed, keep him away from the captain and the first officer, then get him off the boat at the earliest opportunity.

He shook the water from his hands and rubbed them against his pant legs as he strode back inside through the sliding door. He moved quickly, but quietly, hesitating at the corner of the owner's lounge, listening for footsteps or voices on the central stairs beyond. Hearing nothing, he darted around the corner and wound down the stairwell past Paloma's deck and toward the next deck down, where guests were congregated. If he could lose himself in the party, he could play dumb even if the captain were to confront him.

A sound stopped him short, halfway between Paloma's deck and the next. A woman's laughter. Close. Someone was coming. He looked over the curling banister and saw the tips of two pairs of shoes on the steps below him, a man's polished tuxedo shoes and a woman's black pointed heels.

Paul ran back upstairs to Paloma's deck—he didn't dare go up to the owner's deck again—spun in a quick circle, looking for a place to hide. There was the office and the art gallery and the library on one side, but there were no hiding spots in there. If someone came in, Paul would be found immediately. He could go through Paloma's salon and down the stairs to the weather deck below where most of the guests were gathered. But Paloma was likely still in there. And Paul would be seen coming down the stairs from the deck.

Paul cursed under his breath. He hadn't taken the time to explore the rooms on the other half of the deck before he'd snuck upstairs earlier. He didn't know what he would find. But as the voices of the people ascending the stairs grew louder, Paul had run out of time to think it over. He raced to the other side of the lobby and pressed the button beside the first sliding door he encountered.

It didn't open.

He pressed the button again. The door must have been locked.

With no time to think, Paul ran to the next door. Same result. For whatever reason, the doors on this side of the floor were shut. Maybe they were Paloma's private chambers, locked in anticipation of nosy guests like Paul.

The voices coming up the stairs grew even louder, the man's low voice followed by the woman's laughter, like the tinkling of shattered crystal. Paul could see the tops of two heads, one with tousled, dusty-brown hair surrounding a nascent bald spot, the other with diamonds scattered through a raven-colored up-do. They climbed the stairs at a casual pace, probably guests on a self-guided tour. Possibly already drunk and looking for a dark corner for a tryst. Paul could probably talk his way past them, but he'd rather not have to. They would become two more witnesses to tell police they'd seen Paul in an odd location at an inopportune time.

In another five seconds, he wouldn't have a choice. Paul slid along the wall, pressing himself as flat as possible to delay being seen. But it was beginning to feel inevitable. As he slid sideways, he controlled his breathing, composed his face, donned his curious party guest persona.

His hand caught on something. A softening in the wall. A lever. Paul pressed hard and the wall gave way behind him.

Another hidden doorway. The ship was full of them.

Paul moved backwards with the door, eyeing the couple, watching as he closed the door in front of him again. Their focus was on each other. Paul was sure they hadn't noticed him.

He leaned his head against the door and breathed a deep sigh of relief. That had been close. He let his heart rate settle for a moment, then turned in the hallway and looked to see where he was.

Looking back at him were the captain, the first officer, and Paloma Minsk.

13

THE CAPTAIN STOOD in the center of the hallway, his arms crossed over his chest. His face bore the usual stern expression that Paul had gotten used to during his tour. Now, Paul suspected there might be more reason for his sternness than simply being annoyed by a nosy guest.

Behind him stood the first officer. Her arms hung by her side, her stance square, her expression not quite as serious as the captain's, yet somehow even more menacing.

Behind her stood Paloma Minsk, black gown glittering with movie star elegance in the overhead lights. She didn't look stern or serious at all. In fact, she was smiling at Paul.

"I thought I knew how to make an entrance, Mr. Baker," she said, "but maybe you can teach me a few things."

"Turning yourself in?" said the captain drily.

"For what?" responded Paul, doing his best to feign sincere confusion at the question.

The captain snorted. He turned and walked past the first officer and Paloma into the wheelhouse. Paloma laughed at the expression on Paul's face and followed the captain. The first officer held out her hand in a gesture that was at once both welcoming and aggressive. It said to Paul, *You're welcome to join us in the wheelhouse. If you don't, I'll knock you senseless and drag you there myself.* She nodded curtly to Paul as he passed her.

The wheelhouse was empty when Paul stepped in, save for the captain and Paloma speaking quietly in front of the captain's chair. Behind him, the door slid shut. Paul glanced over his shoulder just as the first officer pressed a button to lock the door behind her. She stood like she was guarding it, arms folded across her chest.

Paul walked toward the front bank of controls and scanned out the window. Bright spotlights shined down on the deck, turning the darkness outside the light even darker, making the scene seem more vivid than life, like Paul were watching a movie through the glass.

He had been trying to make his movements look as innocent and casual as possible. He was sure he failed, though, when his mouth fell open in shock at what he saw through the window. Or, rather, what he didn't see.

Minsk's body was gone. Instead, two crew members were under the lights, swabbing the deck with wet mops. A third crew member rinsed it with a hose, steering the water into a drain. The crew had already scrubbed the deck spotless. The water ran bloodless across the floor.

Paul re-composed his face as quickly as he could, but he knew that the others had seen him.

"Something wrong, Mr. Baker?" asked the captain.

"Just amazed at how hard-working your crew is, sir," said Paul. "Scrubbing the deck this late at night? That's dedication for you."

The captain snorted again.

Paloma laughed, the sound surprisingly low and musical. "You're a fun one," she said. "You I like."

Despite the situation, despite himself, Paul couldn't help but feel a warm flush at the flattery from Paloma. One glance at the captain chilled that warmth again in a hurry.

"I had nothing to do with it, I swear," said Paul.

"You had nothing to do with what, Mr. Baker?" said the captain.

Was he looking for a confession? Were they recording him right then? Maybe it was standard practice now to record everything that happened in the wheelhouse of a yacht this size, like the black box in an airplane.

"With what happened," Paul said.

"What happened?" asked the captain.

If he was going to play dumb, then Paul would play dumber.

"I was just looking around, curious. I didn't mean to intrude on Mrs. Minsk's private deck."

The captain sighed deeply and gave a long, slow nod. "I see," he said, then glanced at Paloma.

"No need to apologize, Mr. Baker," said Paloma. "You're welcome any time." She stepped close to him. Paul could smell her perfume, wafting toward him in the wake of her movement. "Will we have the pleasure of your company in the future?"

Paul frowned. What the hell was going on here? The captain and his first officer, who had been standing in front of the locked exit this whole time, watching and listening, had seen him standing at the rail after Minsk had gone over. And now they had him in their wheelhouse.

And yet they weren't interrogating him. Or if they were, it was unlike any interrogation Paul had ever heard of. And they'd already removed the body and were cleaning up the deck.

Wait.

They'd already removed the body and were cleaning up the deck.

That was not something they should have done. They should have immediately turned the ship toward shore, called the harbor police to inform them of the incident, and done what they could to preserve the scene for the cops to investigate. A captain, especially an experienced one like Captain Constance, would have known that.

Paul glanced out the windows, then at the giant electronic map on the wall behind the captain's chair, the one that showed the speed and direction of the yacht.

They hadn't turned around. They weren't headed for shore. They seemed to be following the exact same path they had been all along, skirting the edge of the bay at a leisurely pace.

Even if they hadn't wanted to change course for whatever reason, they could have called the police to come to them. But Paul could see the yellow dots on the map, the ones that represented other ships in the area. They were all clustered close to shore, unmoving. There were no dots coming toward the yacht, certainly nothing that looked like police boats racing to the scene of a high-profile death.

Was this a cover-up? Were they trying to hide Minsk's death? Or were they trying to somehow get Paul to admit to killing him? Or say something they could use to frame him?

Paul eyed the captain and the first officer. The first officer's stoic face told him nothing. It was possible that she didn't know anything. But there was no way Minsk's body could have fallen to the deck in front of the wheelhouse without the first officer knowing about it. If the captain weren't in the wheelhouse, she would have been in charge. And if he were in the wheelhouse, she would have been sitting right in front of the window. Which meant that her stoic expression was a poker face.

Paul made a mental note never to play poker with First Officer Whitley.

The other crew members, the ones who had just stowed their cleaning supplies and disappeared from the deck in front of the windows, would have seen the body, too. Possibly other crew members, as well, if someone else had dragged the body away.

And where would they have taken the body? It had to be here somewhere. They wouldn't have just tossed it over the side. If they hadn't killed him, that would have been a ridiculous thing to do. Even if they were that stupid, which Paul knew they weren't, the body wouldn't just disappear. It would float to shore or be discovered by another vessel. And then they'd have a lot of questions to answer.

Of course, if they had killed him, they'd have even more.

Someone had killed Minsk. And it was someone on this ship. Paul shifted his eyes from the first officer to the captain. There was clearly no love lost between the captain and Minsk. He'd spit on the man's dead body, for chrissakes. Could the captain have murdered Minsk? Would the first officer have done it for him, out of duty or loyalty to her captain? Or did the first officer have her own motive, one that would have led her to murder Minsk on her own volition?

Minsk had a gash on his forehead, a deep one. Bloody. And it looked like he'd been stabbed in the chest, possibly through the heart. But none of those wounds had killed him. They might have, eventually. Especially the chest wound. But it was the fall that had actually killed him. Snapped his neck.

And he'd behaved so strangely before he fell. Not fell. Before he tipped himself over the rail. Was that the result of blood loss and shock? Not just physical shock, but the shock of being attacked and dealt a death blow? Or had he been drugged? What had really been in Minsk's drink before he died?

Regardless of who killed Minsk, the captain, the first officer, and at least three crew members were aware of the death and had taken steps to hide it. Or at least to clean it up. That made them guilty of something. Stupidity, at least. Accessory to murder—or first-degree murder itself—at worst.

And now Paloma was here. The captain had gone to Paloma first. Paul supposed that made some sense. Calling the police first would have made more sense, but informing Paloma of the death of her husband was a close second.

Paul turned his gaze back to Paloma, standing beside him. She smiled back, her expression radiant and welcoming. She certainly didn't seem upset about her husband's death. And Paul couldn't blame her. Minsk was an asshole. But he might have expected a little bit of distress. Surprise, at least. Shock. The man had fallen to his death less than five minutes ago, and yet here she was smiling at Paul like a hostess greeting the guest of honor.

Could Paloma have had something to do with the murder? She'd been on the owner's deck with Minsk earlier that night. Paul had seen her silhouette in the window. And he'd seen Minsk's silhouette, too, moving normally. Paloma had been with him when he was still alive.

And now they wanted to pin it on Paul? If they could get him to confess to something incriminating, or at least suspicious, and get it on record in the wheelhouse recording system, they could bring it to the police in a neat package. Party guest kills wealthy asshole. Intentionally or by accident, who cares? Case closed. Everyone goes home happy.

Except for Paul. Paul would go to prison.

But he wasn't going to fall for that. He'd done nothing wrong, nothing illegal.

Well, not murder, anyway.

But Paul didn't want to have to tell his story, either. The truth would be incriminating in other ways, ways that Paul would prefer not to bring to the attention of the police. In fact, as a general rule, Paul preferred not to deal with the police at all. He had things to do, plans to execute, and the police did not figure into them. Not at this point.

He looked at the faces around him once more, cleared his throat. The captain merely lifted one eyebrow.

"I'd like that, Mrs. Minsk," said Paul.

The captain's eyebrow fell back into place. Paloma slid one arm through Paul's.

"Please, Mr. Baker," she said as she led him away, "call me Paloma."

14

PAUL LET Paloma lead him slowly toward the wheelhouse door and onto the outside deck, the captain moving ahead of them and holding the door open. Paloma nodded once to him as she passed. It seemed to Paul that the nod held more meaning than a simple thank you.

Outside, the wind was softer, warmer than it had been on the deck upstairs. Had they slowed the yacht or simply turned, angled differently against the prevailing breeze? Or was it Paloma on his arm, somehow warming the air around them with her charms? She was a beautiful woman who had been married to a monster for over nine years. Paul had no doubt she would have learned some survival skills in that time. And it was clear that she knew the effect she had on people, especially men, and understood how to use that to her advantage. Paul had to watch himself closely to make sure he wasn't being used in any way he didn't want.

The captain and first officer followed them onto the deck and shut the door behind. Paloma strolled to the front of the wheelhouse with Paul, strolled over the top of the freshly-cleaned spot where Minsk's body had lain just a few minutes earlier.

She didn't miss a step.

She led Paul to the rail at the apex of the curved rail, in front of the wheelhouse. They looked out over the bow deck below, with the red helipad H and a smattering of guests wandering up for the view and the breeze. They were too wealthy, too sophisticated to do the Titanic thing, the Leo and Kate pose on the point of the bow, but Paul was fairly sure at least some of them wanted to. He was sure at least some of them considered themselves to be supermen. They all considered themselves to be kings and queens of the world.

Would any guests have been on the bow when Minsk fell? He didn't recall seeing anyone there from his vantage point up on the owner's deck, but he hadn't really been thinking clearly in that moment. Nonetheless, Paul was sure any guest who witnessed such a thing would have made a scene, would have fainted or cried out or demanded justice or some other kind of self-focusing histrionics. Most likely, they'd all been at the other end of the yacht, listening to Paloma finish her speech.

In fact, the timing had been perfect. Too perfect. Almost like someone had planned for Minsk to die while everyone's attention was occupied elsewhere.

And yet Minsk hadn't been dead when Paul had been there with him by the hot tub. He'd still been alive. Maybe the plan wasn't quite as perfect as it was supposed to be. Maybe the murderer had gotten lucky that Minsk had fallen when he did and where he did. He could as easily have stumbled to the back deck, just above Paloma, and fallen to his death amidst the crowd of guests. That would have put a damper on the fundraising, for sure. Maybe the murder was unplanned, an act of passion in the heat of the moment. Or maybe the murderer was simply careless.

"Why are you here, Mr. Baker?"

"Sorry?" said Paul. Paloma had shaken him from his tangled thoughts.

A flash of anger crossed her eyes, like a shooting star. Or a quick blast from a flamethrower. But it quickly faded, and she smiled indulgently. It was only a momentary lapse, but it was enough. In that moment, Paul realized that deep down, well-controlled and well-hidden beneath that beautiful, refined exterior, Paloma Minsk had a temper. Maybe even a bad one.

Maybe bad enough, after nine long years, to drive her to murder her asshole of a husband.

"You're an investor, you said?"

Paul nodded.

"Then I'm sure you're aware of my husband's companies, of his work. Surely you would have invested before, if you were interested in doing so. Why would you come here, tonight? This is a political fundraiser, after all, not an investment pitch."

Paul shrugged. "Maybe I'm interested in politics."

"Are you?" Paloma smiled, a sly, beguiling smile accompanied by a tilt of her head that made her hair fall over one eye, her other eye gazing up at Paul in a way that stopped his heart. It was no accident. He was sure of that. Paloma had probably made that same movement a hundred times with a hundred men over the years, using it to pry information or favor or whatever else she may have wanted from them.

And damn if it wasn't effective. Even knowing what she was doing, Paul found it hard to resist. His heart skipped four or five beats before he could calm it down.

"I could be," he said. "Or maybe I was just bored, came down to see what all the fuss was about. To meet the famous Devin Minsk." He tilted his head at Paloma, though he was sure it didn't have the same effect on her as she had had on him. "And his equally famous wife."

Paloma laughed once, hard and loud. "I am hardly as famous as my husband."

Paul looked straight ahead, spoke to the wind. "He may be more infamous," he said, "but I think you're more famous."

When he turned back to her, Paloma's head was tilted again, but not in a calculated way. This time she seemed to be considering him more seriously.

"Then you're aware of my husband's... less savory dealings?"

"I'm aware of the rumors."

"The reputation, you mean?"

"They're usually earned."

Paul smiled at Paloma. She smiled back.

"He was not a good man," Paloma said, her smile dissolving into a pensive expression, her brow creased and her eyes clouded with memory. "Not as bad as the rumors. Not anymore, at least. Not since I've known him. He encouraged the rumors more than he acted them out. But, still, he was not a good man."

"Not a good husband?"

"What's the difference?" Paloma shrugged. "Some women would have been happy enough. Wealth and freedom is all some women need."

"But you need more."

"I *want* more." That flame was back in her eyes, but this time is was not directed outward, not directed at Paul. It reflected an intensity inside her. "I'm worthy of more."

"Why did you marry him, then?"

Paloma scoffed. "Are you an investor or a reporter, Mr. Baker?"

"Just curious."

"I was young, and he was dashing."

"Quite a bit older than you."

"Quite a bit wealthier than my father. I think that's all my father saw. A path to prosperity."

"For himself?"

"For his daughter."

"Didn't you have a say in it?"

"Of course I did," said Paloma, that fire in her voice now, not just in her eyes. "I came from a small town, but my father was no simpleton. He was an educated man. An open-minded man. *He* was a *good* man. He didn't force me to marry like some other fathers might have done, like some of my friends' fathers did. *I* chose this path."

Paul nodded slowly. "Did you know what you were choosing?"

Paloma's mouth pressed into a line. She looked away, into the night. "No. Not really."

"Would you change your decision, if you could do it again?"

She hesitated for a moment, then looked at Paul again, her face serious. "No. Not really."

"Why not?"

Paloma was quiet for a moment. "Are you a religious man, Mr. Baker?"

"No."

"Have you read the bible, at least?"

"No, I haven't."

"Then you're like most people who quote it." She gave a fluttering, apologetic smile. "I was raised Catholic. We read the bible every night before bed."

"Sounds very Spanish."

"Yes, well, what was no so typically Spanish was the Camus and the Voltaire and the Sartre that my father would read to us as we fell asleep."

"After the bible."

Paloma nodded. "Most people quote the bible as saying that money is the root of all evil. And it does say that. First Timothy, chapter six."

"Okay."

"But what they fail to mention—or fail to even realize, I don't know which—is that the quote comes from the middle of the sentence. There are words that come before it. What Timothy actually says is that the love of money is the root of all evil."

"I see."

"So I would choose this path again, not because of my husband, but because of his money. And not because I love the money. He loved the money. These people here," she gestured behind her, toward the party at the back of the ship, "they love money. Or, to be precise, they love the sense of importance they think money brings them."

"And you don't?"

"I hate it. I hate the feeling that people aren't being genuine around me because they know my husband is wealthy. People without money act differently around people with money. They don't act like their true selves. And most people with money don't even know who their true selves are."

"You seem to know yourself pretty well, and you've got money."

The ship turned slightly, turned toward the prevailing winds coming off the open sea. A gust blew Paloma's hair across her face, obscuring it. She turned into the wind, letting it blow the hair back off of her face. Her hair streamed in a plume behind her head, like the unfurling of a standard. For a fleeting moment, Paul had the image in his mind of a warrior queen riding at a gallop, leading her army into battle. When Paloma tucked her hair behind one ear and turned toward him again, the image vanished, snaking away on the breeze.

"We argued," she said softly, her voice almost lost in a gust. "More and more over the years. As I got older. Wiser."

"You argued about money?"

"I don't like these kinds of things," she gestured dismissively toward the yacht, like she was throwing torn bread to a group of bickering seagulls. "These displays of wealth. Do you know how much this yacht cost?"

Paul had an idea, but he shrugged.

"A hundred million dollars." She raised her eyebrows in astonishment. "That amount of money would feed every family in my hometown for the rest of their lives. And then some. And instead, we're doing this, floating in a pond begging for more money from more rich people."

"So you want to use the money differently?"

"I want to help people. Not idiots who don't know how lucky they are. Real people. People who would be grateful to live a peaceful life, without struggle. Who would feel fortunate to know that their next meal will be there for them when they want it. People who eat when they're hungry, not when the clock tells them to or when a plate of food is in front of them."

"Is that why you killed your husband?" said Paul.

It was a rude thing to say, and a risky thing. Paul wasn't sure why he said it, even after the words had left his lips. But as soon as he did, he wanted to hear the answer.

Paul had never seen a smile like the one on Paloma's face in that moment. Part amusement, part confusion, part calculation. Part anger, even. The flames in her eyes licked and leaped and sparked in the night.

"That's why I'm not upset that you killed him, Mr. Baker," she said. "You've done the world—and me—a favor." She tilted her head at Paul again, again gazing up at him through her hair with one sparking eye. "But I doubt the police will see it that way."

This time, it wasn't her gaze that stopped Paul's heart.

15

PAUL STARED BACK AT PALOMA, his mind reeling. The breeze from the open sea kicked into a stiff wind, slapping his cheek with a cold hand, leaving it stinging. The smell of rotting fish filled his nose for a moment before it blew away.

"I didn't kill your husband," he said.

Paloma put on a confused expression. "There are several witnesses," she glanced over her shoulder at the captain and first officer, standing a few paces away, "who say they saw you push him over the rail onto the deck." She stepped back and made a show of looking at her feet. "This deck right here."

The captain came and stood beside Paloma, summoned by her glance.

"Is everything all right?" he said, his gruff, faintly-accented voice laced with poison.

"Just a casual accusation of murder," Paul replied. "*False* accusation."

Paloma and the captain stared back at Paul, neither saying anything. Paul was waiting for the captain to arrest him, to handcuff him to a drainpipe in one of the storage rooms in the lower decks or something like that.

But he didn't. He hadn't. Yet.

They still hadn't called the police. The captain and first officer had been with Paul and Paloma the whole time. Paul would have noticed if one of them had slipped away to radio for help. And they weren't that far from shore. Just a few miles. The police boats would have arrived by now if they'd been called.

No, there was something else going on here. They were threatening to pin this death on Paul, threatening to turn him over to the police, but going to great pains to let him think that without coming out and saying it.

And yet they were also doing everything they could to cover up the death. They'd already moved the body. To where, Paul didn't know. And now they were trying to blackmail him into... what? Into silence? Into confessing and turning himself in?

"If you think I killed him," Paul said, "why aren't you locking me up? Shouldn't you be taking me into custody, calling the police, that sort of thing?"

"I'd be happy to lock you up," said the captain.

Paloma rested one hand on the captain's forearm and smiled, a brilliant, charming smile that lit the night, as if the captain had made a hilarious joke instead of a menacing threat. "There's no need to lock anyone up," she said. "We're on a boat in the middle of the water, after all. And we're all civilized people."

The way the captain stared at Paul was anything but civilized.

"Right, Mr. Baker?" Paloma pressed, raising her eyebrows at Paul.

Paul ignored the prompt. "In other words, you don't feel the need to lock me up because there's no way for me to escape."

Paloma smiled again, but this time, the flames in her eyes dampened the effect. "Sometimes there's a difference between following the law and doing what's right. We're giving you a chance to do what's right."

Paul stared back at her and the captain, keeping his face as expressionless as possible. But in his own mind, he was confused as hell. He couldn't figure out what they were trying to say to him. Were they threatening to turn him into the police? Surely, they knew he hadn't killed Minsk. Maybe one of them had done it. If so, were they telling him to keep his mouth shut or they'd pin the murder on him? Or were they telling him they were going to pin it on him no matter what? Or were they actually trying to get him to turn himself in for a murder he didn't commit? Maybe they hadn't killed Minsk and they really did think he'd done it.

Paul realized that it didn't matter to him what they thought or what they were trying to say. He had no intention of going to the police, either as a scapegoat or as a snitch.

He understood why they didn't want to call the cops. Nothing put a damper on a fundraiser more than bringing justice to the front of people's minds. Half of the moneybags on board probably earned their fortunes by breaking the law, or at least bending it. No one liked be reminded of that fact.

But he had no idea why they would be willing to let him roam the ship freely. The smart thing would be to lock him up, wait until they docked, and spin the police their story before Paul had a chance to tell his side. By letting him roam freely, he could spread the word that Minsk was dead, start a rumor that one of them had done it. It was a dumb play, and he didn't think Paloma or the captain were dumb people. Which meant they had some other motive for not locking him up.

But Paul wasn't one to look a gift horse in the mouth. And being free to roam the ship meant he was free to figure out what really happened to Minsk, then use that information to flip the tables on whoever really killed him.

Right now, the top suspects were Captain William Constance, First Officer Whitley, and Mrs. Paloma Minsk. Whether they worked together to kill him or not, they were certainly working together to hide his death. Or at least obscure the truth about it.

Paul looked from Paloma to the captain and back again. "Okay," he said. "I'll keep my mouth shut."

"I knew you would understand," said Paloma, slipping her arm through Paul's and leading him across the deck again to the other side of the wheelhouse. Her body was warm, and her curves pressed against Paul's side in very distracting ways as she pushed through the wheelhouse door, out the back, and down the hallway. "I felt a connection between us the moment we met, like we'd known each other for years. Maybe in a past life."

She pushed through the hidden door at the end of the hallway and stood at the landing of the curved central staircase. She turned to face Paul, put one hand on his cheek, soft and warm. "I knew in that moment we'd become good friends." She kissed him on one cheek, then the other, slow kisses from her full lips.

Even after the threats out on the deck, Paul's stomach still flipped at her touch, and he felt faint, dazed. Paloma must have noticed—or expected—the response. She smiled, her eyes twinkling and mischievous. "Go," she said softly. "Enjoy the party."

Still in a daze, Paul turned dutifully and stepped down the stairs as if in a dream, one halting, jerking step at a time. When his senses finally began to come back to him, several steps down, he turned and looked back up at where Paloma had stood.

She was already gone.

16

PAUL WAS STILL HALF-DAZED and emotionally fevered when the sliding door opened in front of him and he wandered through into the salon on Deck Four. The crowd around him was chattering and loud. Paul heard a flare of laughter as some wag or another made a joke that his companions felt obliged to laugh at. As he walked, his daze faded and his fever increased. He felt like he was walking through a nightmare, surrounded by handkerchiefs and hair plugs, Botox and boob jobs.

He veered to one side to stand at a tall table covered with a cluster of empty champagne flutes, wine glasses, and tumblers that had yet to be cleared. Paul didn't care about the mess. All he cared about was that there were no people standing there. He could stop and collect himself. It was a few minutes more before his surroundings soaked through his Paloma-induced brain haze and chilled him closer to his right mind.

Paloma Minsk was a weapon far more dangerous that anything her husband had ever sold.

Her *late* husband. Someone on this yacht had killed Devin Minsk. And Paul had to figure out who it was before the ship returned to the dock, or he'd be spending the next few days in an interrogation room explaining himself to the cops.

And if that happened, Paul would have a lot of explaining to do. A hell of a lot more than just about Devin Minsk, and a hell of a lot more than he wanted. There was no way he would let that happen. He'd gotten on board to do a job, not to get caught up in a murder scheme.

And yet somehow he hadn't done the job yet, and he'd not only gotten caught up in the scheme, he was set up to take the fall for a murder he didn't commit.

As far as nights go, so far it wasn't Paul's best.

"Enjoying the party so far?"

It took Paul a long moment to recognize the woman who had come up to his table. He stared blankly at her, her beautiful face adrift in his memory, searching for a place to dock.

She frowned at him, then scanned the table and laughed.

"Looks like you're either enjoying it too much or not enough," she said. "Maybe you should slow down a little."

"Melantha," said Paul, the face finally finding its berth. He shook his head. "Sorry, I... My mind is a little preoccupied at the moment."

"Preoccupied or plastered?" She gestured toward the table. "These all yours?"

"No," said Paul. "Not mine."

"Then I'd say you need a drink." Melantha raised her chin at someone. A server in a white shirt and black necktie came over, tray in hand. "My friend here needs a drink. What'll you have, Paul? It is Paul, right?"

Paul nodded. "Rye, neat. Thank you."

"May I get you anything, miss?" said the server as he cleared the empty glasses from the table onto his tray.

Melantha raised a tumbler cradled in her hand, wrapped in a white cocktail napkin soaked with condensation. "I'm fine, thanks."

"What's got you so preoccupied?" said Melantha when the server had gone. "Too much excitement for you?"

Paul laughed. If only she knew. "I don't know," he lied. "Seasick, maybe?"

"Hmm. Yeah. Pretty nautical out. Those waves have got to be pushing two feet. I'm surprised anyone is still standing."

"Fair point," Paul nodded. "I guess I just got lost in thought for a minute." He smiled at her. She smiled back, and the last vestiges of that Paloma-induced brain haze were gone for good. "What do *you* think of the party?"

"I think it's exactly what I thought it would be. A bunch of boring people doing a bunch of boring shit on an overpriced boat in the middle of the bay."

Paul laughed. "Then why are you here?"

"Maybe I'm boring, too."

"I can put that thought to rest for you. You're definitely not boring."

"How would you know? Maybe you're even more boring than me, so I look exciting by comparison."

Paul opened his mouth to respond, then thought about it for a second and closed his mouth again. There was really no way to counter that line of thinking.

Melantha laughed. "Now you'll be spending the rest of the night re-evaluating all of your opinions."

"Nah," Paul said. "My opinions aren't that important."

"You might be the only person here who thinks that way about themselves."

"Including you?"

"Definitely," she said. "I have a very high opinion of myself. It's my greatest fault."

"And also your greatest strength?"

"You got it." Her smile made Paul smile back. He couldn't help it.

"So why are you here, then, really?" Paul said. "Are you an investor? Business owner? You couldn't possibly be a politician."

"Would that be so bad?" She smiled, then shook her head. "No, I'm nobody special. I'm just here with someone."

Paul's stomach fell, his smile faltering just a touch before he propped it back up again. "Oh, okay. Your husband? Boyfriend?"

"Why not girlfriend?"

"Okay," Paul laughed. "So are you here with your girlfriend?"

"None of the above," said Melantha. "I guess you could call them my ex."

"You came to a party on a yacht with your ex? That's brave."

"What better way to get back at an ex than to fuck them over in front of a bunch of rich assholes?"

"Damn," said Paul. "Remind me not to get on your bad side."

The server arrived with Paul's drink. He set two cocktail napkins on the table and put Paul's drink on one of them. A generous serving, three fingers of rich caramel-colored rye whiskey in a smooth-sided tumbler. He didn't anticipate anything near as good as what Paloma had served him earlier, but his mouth watered at the sight, all the same. He didn't realize how much he needed a drink.

"I don't have a bad side," said Melantha. "My ex was a two-timing asshole who deserved what he got. So don't call it a bad side. It's justice, baby."

Paul raised his glass. "To justice."

Melantha wadded up the soaked-through napkin from around her tumbler and dropped it on the table. She held her glass up beside Paul's. "To past exes," she winked at him, "and future ones."

She clinked his glass and they both sipped. As the scotch slid over his tongue and down his throat, as he watched Melantha drink across the table from him, Paul noticed two things.

First, the diamond necklace Melantha had been wearing on the ferry was gone. Her neck was bare. Beautiful, smooth, and long, but bare.

And second, the tumbler she held, that she tipped against

the dark red lipstick on her sultry lips, wasn't like Paul's. Paul's tumbler had smooth sides. Melantha's didn't. Hers had an unusual off-kilter octagonal cut.

Ice clinked in Paul's glass, and ran down Paul's spine.

While he sipped, Paul glanced around the room at the glasses in the hands of the other guests. Those who held tumblers held ones like Paul's, with smooth sides. Melantha's was the only one with that strange cut to the crystal.

Paul had seen the off-kilter octagonal cut before. In Minsk's office, where two such tumblers were missing from the shelf in his bar.

And in Minsk's hand just before he died.

His heartbeat thumped in his ears as he looked over the rim of his glass at Melantha.

He swallowed his whiskey, but he didn't taste it at all.

17

PAUL SET his drink back down on the table and scanned the room, watching the well-dressed wealthy becoming increasingly drunk and loud. He tried to appear casual even as his mind raced, playing out the possible timelines in his mind.

Melantha had boarded the yacht before Paul, and he hadn't seen her since the ferry. He'd been off on his own adventure, so there was no way for him to know where Melantha had been. But she surely had time to go upstairs, kill Minsk, and be back before Paul got to the salon. Plenty of time for that.

But what about Paloma? And the other guy, the accountant, Vernon Stratham? Could she have avoided them? He ran through the events of the last two hours in his mind. He'd been on Deck Five outside the wheelhouse with the captain maybe an hour after boarding. He'd seen Paloma in the window on Deck Six, the owner's deck, seen Minsk come up to her. Minsk had been alive then.

Then he'd wound up in Paloma's art gallery and library, maybe ten minutes later. Ten minutes after that, he'd seen Stratham walking up the central staircase to the owner's deck, right before he ran into Paloma. Spent time with her, maybe

98

twenty minutes, ending with that drink in her salon when Stratham came back downstairs.

And then he'd gone up to the owner's deck himself. Slipped into the office, maybe fifteen minutes, tops. Then ten minutes exploring the rest of the deck before finding Minsk.

The whole time from when he'd seen Minsk alive with Paloma to when he'd found him dying on the upper deck was no more than an hour, hour and ten minutes. And for half of that time, Stratham had been with Minsk. Could Melantha have gone up in the five minutes while Stratham was in the salon with Paloma and Paul, before Paul went up to the office? Could she have poured two drinks, inflicted two deadly wounds, and slipped back downstairs without running into Paul? Without him even hearing her?

"What do you think?" said Melantha.

"What? About what?" said Paul, too quickly, too sharply.

Melantha just smiled at him. "About your drink. Good?"

"Oh, yeah, yeah." Paul took another quick sip. "Hits the spot."

She laughed. "Well, go easy," she said. "I don't want you getting preoccupied on me again." Her smile was a sly one.

Paul laughed back, a thin, weak laugh that sounded completely fake to his ears. He just hoped Melantha didn't notice.

He pointed at her glass. "What are you drinking?"

"Vodka," she said. "I think. I didn't really ask. My ex gave it to me."

She flagged the server down and asked him to bring her some ice for her drink. Paul shook his head when the server asked if he wanted his glass topped off.

Her ex? Could Melantha have been dating Minsk?

The server returned and dropped two ice cubes in Melantha's glass. "I'm really not much of a drinker," she said. "Never liked the taste. But at a party like this, you have to have something in your hand. If I get a drink at the start and keep adding ice, I can nurse it for the whole party and not have to answer any stupid questions."

Paul nodded, his mind in shock.

"It's more water than vodka at this point."

Paul sipped his drink again.

"Am I boring you? Keeping you from something more interesting?"

"What?" said Paul. "Of course not. What do you mean?"

"As much as I like listening to myself talk, I was hoping for a little more interaction when I came over here." She smiled as she said it, but Paul could see the annoyance in Melantha's eyes, could hear it in her voice.

"Sorry," he said. "I'm sorry. I was just—"

"Preoccupied?"

He winced and nodded. "Tell you what. I'm going to use the restroom." He jabbed his thumb over his shoulder, then pointed at the deck behind Melantha. "Why don't I meet you out on deck? It's a little too stuffy in here."

She stared at him for a long moment, one eyebrow raised. "Fine," she said at last. She pulled the dry cocktail napkin from the table and wrapped it around her glass before picking it up. "I'll see you out there."

She turned, took one long slow step, then paused. Her golden dress cascaded off her shoulder, flowed around her bare back, then met to cradle the curve of her hips. From there it flowed behind one bare leg—bent to expose nearly its full, voluptuous length—and down to the floor. She looked back over her shoulder at Paul. "Don't keep me waiting," she said.

She was a vision straight from the cover of a magazine, and she knew it. Paul watched her stride away, slipping between groups of guests and through the door to the deck outside. Her silky dress caressed her, her bare leg slipping in and out of view as she walked. The cut of the gorgeous gown accentuated

Melantha's even more gorgeous hourglass figure. The view stopped Paul's heart.

Paul shook his head and slugged back the rest of his drink. It was bad enough that he was such a sucker for a beautiful woman. But why was it that every beautiful woman he met wound up being a suspect for murder?

18

PAUL WENT OUT of the Deck Four salon to the vestibule around the central staircase. An older couple was coming up from Deck Three, winding arm-in-arm around the curve of the stair. Paul made a pretense of checking his phone until they had gone past him into the party. Glancing around again to be sure he was alone, he dashed up the stairs, taking them two at a time, stepping as lightly as possible on the balls of his feet so as not to make a sound on the marble stairs.

He didn't stop as he passed Deck Five, just hoped that no one was there to see him blow by. He didn't notice anyone as he climbed. Maybe Paloma was still in the wheelhouse with the captain, or back in her salon. Or maybe she was doing her duty and schmoozing with the guests on the lower decks, making excuses for her husband's absence and encouraging the guests to donate generously.

Paul didn't know and he didn't care. He wanted to get back upstairs and have another look around before the captain had his cleaning crew set to work on it. He just hoped they hadn't done it already.

He paused for a moment at the top of the stairs, listening for sounds of movement as he had the first time he'd gone up there, extending his senses to try to feel if anyone else was nearby. He heard nothing, felt nothing.

That seemed weird to Paul. If the captain had cleaned up the body so quickly, the next obvious move would be to clean up the place where the body had come from.

But maybe he'd already finished. Only one way to find out.

Paul pulled in a deep breath, then moved around the corner as he let it out slowly, letting his muscles relax as the breath flowed out of him. He dashed through the owner's lounge, scanning it quickly for anything out of place, and out the sliding door onto the deck with the hot tub, the bow deck where Minsk had tipped himself over the rail.

The tumbler was still there, laid on its side, scraping softly back and forth against the wood flooring as the ship rocked in the waves of the bay. Paul wished he had brought a pair of gloves. There was probably a medical kit somewhere that would have some, maybe even a full medical bay. But he didn't have time to search the whole yacht for them. He would have to make do with his shirt sleeves.

He pulled out his cuff links and stashed them in his jacket pocket, then unfolded the cuff and tucked his hands back within them. Using the cuff as a makeshift glove, he picked up the tumbler. He sniffed it. It didn't smell like much of anything at all, which didn't surprise Paul. If Minsk had been drinking vodka, it wouldn't leave much of a scent behind.

He held the tumbler up to the light coming from under the seats. The glass seemed cloudy, like there was a residue there. Straight vodka wouldn't leave a residue, especially expensive Russian vodka that was—what had the bottle said?—*impressively pure and smooth*. And the deck was too tall for a rogue splash of sea water to have hit the glass and dried. Maybe the salt air could have left a haze on the glass, but not in the forty-five minutes or so since Minsk had dropped it.

Paul hesitated for a moment, then slid the back of one bare

knuckle around the inside of the glass, along the residue. He could see a clear line in the light where he'd wiped the cloudiness clear. He sniffed his knuckle, then touched it to his tongue.

He spit, pushing his tongue out over and over to scrape the tip clean with his teeth. The residue tasted bitter, chemical. Paul got down on his hands and knees and sniffed the deck where Minsk had spilled his drink. He got down low, almost laying down so he could see the wood of the deck against the light from under the seats. He saw the faint glossy stain of the drink, then saw the matte dullness where a residue had been left behind. Paul had no doubt that if he licked the deck in that spot he'd taste the same chemical bitterness he'd gotten from the inside of the tumbler.

He was no expert, but if Paul had to guess, he'd say that someone had poisoned Minsk's drink earlier that night.

He put the tumbler in his pocket, used the hot tub to wash the residue from his knuckle, and went back inside to the office. He pulled out the bottle of vodka, the one whose label had been turned backwards earlier, and poured it into a fresh tumbler. He sniffed it. Paul didn't get any of the *notes of vanilla, sage, white pepper, and cream* promised by the label on the bottle, but it smelled clean. Like good vodka.

He swirled the liquid around in the tumbler a bit, let it settle, swirled it again. If the whole bottle was poisoned, Paul didn't know if it were activated by the heat from his hand or if it took a while to activate when it met the air or what. Or maybe it was just good old-fashioned arsenic or something. Hemlock. Something that would just plain kill you when you drank it. Hoping he'd waited long enough, he poured the vodka down the sink and held the glass up to the light.

There was a residue. Paul tasted it, then spat it out in the wet bar's sink and rinsed his finger under the tap. Same bitter, chemical taste.

Minsk had been poisoned.

That might explain his mental state, the dreamy, drowsy, semi-catatonic mental state he'd shown on the deck. It might even explain the sudden shift to aggressiveness, when he nearly broke Paul's arm. Maybe that was what this kind of poison did to you as it slowly worked its way through your body. Maybe it drove you nuts so you killed yourself. That might give the killer plausible deniability. *He threw himself off the side of the yacht and drowned, your honor, while I was off grifting our rich guests.* Might not hold up with a tox report, but if the poison didn't stay in the system for very long, maybe it could work.

But the poison hadn't been Minsk's only problem. He had a nasty gash on his forehead. Probably not enough to bleed him out, but not something you'd want to walk around with, either. Maybe he'd tripped and fallen, banged his head on a desk or a counter in his drugged state. If so, there would be evidence somewhere, blood stains on a carpet or smears on a table edge.

And what about the chest wound? That one was definitely a killer, and definitely not accidental. Someone had delivered that blow, unless Minsk had suddenly decided to off himself with a pair of scissors to the heart. Either way, with that much blood, there had to be some physical evidence.

Paul peeked through the office curtain. Seeing no one out there, he slipped into the passageway and through to the bedroom. The bed was made, tight and tucked. It showed no sign that anyone had sat or lain there.

Paul pulled off the pillows, one by one, looked them over. No signs of blood. No tears or cuts on them. He tugged down the covers. Same with the sheets. The bed looked clean. He put everything back together the way he'd found it.

Next he examined the outside of the room. On the left side of the bed hung a flat-screen television. A big one. And one with corners that were sharp enough to leave a nasty gash in some-one's head if they fell—or were pushed—against it hard enough. He checked the sides and corners for traces of blood. Nothing.

He even turned the TV on. It still worked fine, tuned to a Russian business channel with international market prices scrolling the chyrons at the bottom of the screen. Turns out the lingua franca of the world wasn't English at all. It was money.

The sliding door to the owner's deck opened with a soft hiss. Paul stepped through, slow and cautious. He immediately heard chatter from the guests below, the soft sound of nondescript piano jazz being played or piped in. He wanted to check the deck for evidence, but he definitely did not want anyone below to see him.

The flames were still lit in the firepit between the couch and chairs. The couch and chairs were soft, with no hard edges that could cause the kind of wounds Paul had seen on Minsk's face. The table with the firepit in the center might have. A solid elongated rectangle with rounded edges and sides, it looked like the barrel of a rifle laying on the deck. Paul ran his hands along it, tried to shift it. The thing was too heavy to move. Seemed to be made of solid granite. Could definitely leave a mark if you whacked your head against it.

The firepit in the center was lit, low and steady, putting off enough light for Paul to examine the edge of the table all around. It was also hot enough to make Paul's face burn as he did so, the skin tightening around his eyes and over his cheeks from the heat. He examined the entire edge of the table, his face inches away, and saw nothing. No chips or irregularities in the granite. No blood stains or flecks of dried blood. Nothing.

He ran along the rail in the same fashion, trying to be as quick and unobtrusive as possible. Hard to do with a glass rail. Paul had no choice but to move fast and hope no one below happened to look up two decks and see him.

He found nothing unusual on the rail either. No blood, no chips or cracks in the glass, no dents in the gold top rail. If Minsk's head wounds came from banging against something, it didn't happen on the aft deck.

Paul moved back inside. The sliding doors shut behind him, shutting out the sounds of the crowd and the party. He felt an immediate sense of relief at the quiet that wrapped him like a blanket. He was still exposed up here on the owner's deck. If someone found him, he'd have to do some serious tap dancing to get out of it. But at least he wasn't outside under the potential eyes of a hundred guests.

He resumed his search, checking the ashtray on the table beside the sliding door. The cigar had burned itself out completely by now, nothing but a rickety grey ash-shadow of its former Cuban glory, laying in the ashtray like the sloughed skin of a very short and remarkably cylindrical snake. Paul ruined the tableau when he picked up the ashtray with his shirt cuff and examined it under the light, looking for any trace of blood. There was none there, either.

Bathroom next. Like stepping into the executive washroom at Fort Knox. Paul felt like a pharaoh as he examined the gold faucets, the gold sconces, the gold-veined marble of the countertop for any signs of blood or struggle. The bathroom was as clean as everywhere else had been. Paul pushed out a heavy sigh, trying to rein in his increasing frustration. He needed evidence, some clue as to who actually did this, so that he could fling it in Paloma's face and the captain's face the next time they tried to blackmail him.

The dressing room was across the passageway from the bathroom. Paul moved in that direction, then stopped as he heard voices coming up the stairs. He couldn't make them out. A man's voice, low. Then a woman's.

Someone was coming. And Paul had nowhere to hide.

19

PAUL STOOD in the center of the bathroom and closed his eyes. As the sound of the voices grew louder, nearer, he controlled his breathing, focused on his hearing. The owner's deck was one long oval passageway along the outside edge, moving from the lounge and the hot tub deck at the bow to the bedroom and the larger deck aft and back again. In the center were the staircase and the bathroom, with the straight-line passageway of the bathroom providing the only shortcut across the oval. From where he stood, if Paul could figure out which side of the oval the two voices were coming from, he might be able to slip out the other side of the shortcut and escape undetected.

His panic was high in his throat, constricting it, pinging his ears with a high whine that made it hard for him to tell the direction of the voices. He practiced a calming breathing pattern, breathing in, holding it, breathing out, waiting, then repeating the cycle. The pulse pounding in his neck slowed. The whine in his ears receded.

The voices were coming from Paul's right, down the passageway from the stairs, getting louder as they moved past the office toward the bedroom. Paul ran on soft feet over the gold-flecked bathroom tile into the passageway on the other side. He pressed his back against the wall, waiting to confirm that the voices would go to the bedroom.

"...not illegal, really, just irregular," said the first voice, the man's voice. It sounded like Stratham, the accountant. "Most of the guests would have come to see Mr. Minsk in person, if not the Attorney General himself."

"And you think they'll be disappointed if they don't see him?"

That voice was Paloma's. Paul heard it clearly as they approached the door on the other side of the bathroom.

"Possibly."

"And you think that will decrease their donations."

Stratham chuckled. "Possibly. But the Attorney General has no shortage of donors or donations. More importantly, it's Mr. Minsk that is the designated proxy for the fundraiser. If he isn't here, there may be some legal concerns that the PAC would need to deal with. I'd like to try to prevent that..."

They continued into the bedroom, the sound of their voices muffled by the bulkhead. Paul dashed down the passageway in the other direction, grateful for the thick pile carpet that muted the sound of his footsteps. He would need to run all the way around the oval—down the length of the deck, through the lounge at the other end and around to the stairwell again—in order to get away. Hopefully, whatever Paloma and Stratham were doing in the bedroom would take at least a few minutes.

A cool breeze coming from the far end of the passageway slowed him. A glimpse of movement stopped him short just before the opening into the lounge. He crouched down and crept forward. Fortunately, there was no sliding door at the end of the passageway on this side of the lounge. He could move ahead without the hiss of an opening door to announce his presence.

Peering around the bulkhead, Paul saw people on the bow deck. He recognized the blond hair and stolid stance of the First Officer Whitley as she stood in the doorway, her back to Paul.

The breeze he'd felt was coming through the open door. Paul could smell the salt in the air, could smell the chlorine from the hot tub, still burbling happily on the deck. Beyond the first officer, Paul could see two crew members, their backs bent over long-handled mops, their white uniform shirts glowing in the light as they scrubbed the deck clean under their first officer's sharp eye.

Paul leaned back against the wall of the passageway. On the one hand, he was glad he'd been able to get up to the bow deck before the crew, to get the tumbler and discover that Minsk's drink had been poisoned. On the other hand, now he was trapped in a passageway with only two exits. Paloma and the accountant were on one end. The first officer and two of her crew were on the other end. Unless he wanted to jump out the window, Paul's only way out was past one of those two groups.

Paul let out a long, silent breath and lay his head back against the wall. He could hear the first officer ordering her crew around. He knew she would come down his passageway eventually. He had no doubt that she would make sure the top deck was thoroughly cleaned.

He could take his chances, wait there and hope she worked in the other direction, moving toward the office and around through the bedroom with her cleaning crew. That would give Paul a chance to slip downstairs unseen.

But there was an equal chance that she'd come in his direction first. If she did that, he would be caught. No excuses. No leniency. They would handcuff him to the drainpipe for sure.

If he ran the other way, back toward the bedroom, he could hope that Paloma and Stratham were out on the deck or otherwise occupied, allowing him to slip through the bathroom to the other side. But he'd still have to make it all the way down the passageway to the stairwell before the first officer and her crew found him. That was a long way to go, and a lot of risk to take.

Paul tapped the back of his head softly against the bulkhead behind him. He had no options, but he had to do something. If he stayed put, he'd be caught for sure.

A cool gust carried through the open door from the lounge and past Paul. He eyed the windows again. Did they even open? He thought back to the view from outside, when he'd been on the deck below with the captain. The superstructure had looked smooth and unclimbable from down there, but maybe there were footholds from this angle.

He stood and examined the windows. The first two were smaller, triangular windows. They were fixed, with no way to open them, but the next one had a small latch. Paul flipped it open and pushed at the window with the side of his hand. It slid open easily, a gust of cool, wet wind smacking Paul in the face.

He poked his head out. There was a small lip about three inches wide that ran along the bottom of the windows, almost the full length of the passageway. The smooth white superstructure arched down from above the windows, ending in a point at either end. A few feet beyond that on either side were the rails for the decks, the bow deck to Paul's right, where the first officer and her crew were cleaning, and the aft deck far down to his left, outside the bedroom that Paloma and Stratham had entered.

The window wasn't huge, but Paul could get through it. The problem was, he couldn't just crouch there on the lip of the superstructure and wait. If anyone looked out the window as they walked down the passageway, they'd see him. He would have to shimmy along the length of the lip under the window and figure out a way to hide himself until everyone went down below.

Not a great option.

But a bad option was better than no option at all. And Paul didn't have many options left.

He took a deep breath and hoisted one leg through the open window.

20

OF ALL THE ideas Paul had had in his life, this was definitely not one of his best.

He clung spread-eagled to the outside of a yacht at sea, at least forty feet above dark, cold water, five miles from shore, straddling part of the yacht's aluminum superstructure.

Three toes of his left foot—that's all he could fit—dug into the aluminum lip under the last window of the row along the passageway. His right foot pressed against the side of the smooth superstructure, with only the hard sole of his dress shoe for traction. His left hand scrabbled for a grip on the underside of the window overhang, holding on by the tips of his fingers, his finger joints squeezed into tents. His right hand was the only part of him that had anything resembling a firm hold, clutching the superstructure where it curled flat toward the rail of the aft deck outside the owner's bedroom.

If a drone were to fly by at that moment, Paul would have looked exactly like a bug that had splatted on a windshield, provided the windshield were the side of a hundred-million-dollar megayacht.

As precarious as his position was, it turned out to have been a good decision to go out the window. As he pressed his right cheek against the cold aluminum of the yacht's superstructure, he could see the first officer and her crew through the windows in the passageway he'd just left. Fortunately, he'd managed to close the window behind him, otherwise they would have investigated. They would have stuck their heads out and spotted Bugsplat Paul immediately.

Unfortunately, because he'd closed the window, he couldn't hear anything they were saying.

And even more unfortunately, Paul watched as one of the crew members stopped and, with a slight frown, clicked the lock on the inside of the window. Going back inside the way he'd come out was no longer an option for Paul.

While the first officer and crew were in the passageway, cleaning as they worked their way toward the bedroom, Paloma and Stratham were on the aft deck outside the bedroom, to Paul's right. From this vantage, Paul now knew that if he'd gone back to the bathroom and cut through to the other side, he could have been down at the party by now, bored out of his mind instead of scared out of his mind clinging to the side of the yacht. But, hindsight and so on...

He flipped his head, pressing his left cheek against the side of the yacht. Because of the angle, he couldn't see Paloma and Stratham unless they happened to lean over the side rail. Like the crew members in the hallway, if they did that they would see the Paul-splat and the jig would be up. Paul would spend the rest of the cruise cuffed to a drainpipe and the next fifteen to twenty-five years in prison.

From the dull sound of their voices, though, he was pretty sure they were either sitting on the chairs in the middle of the deck or standing at the back rail. He could hear them talking, but no matter how much he strained his ears, he couldn't make out what they were saying over the wind and the waves and the faint tinkle of champagne glasses and piano jazz.

The yacht jarred against a set of tall rollers, jouncing Paul.

His right shoe slipped, his hand squeaked as the skin slid along the aluminum superstructure. His heart tried to leap out of his chest to save itself and wound up hammering in his temples instead.

The ship settled on the water again, resumed its gentle rise and fall. Paul reset his footing, tried to calm his breathing to match the rhythm of the waves. Slowly, his heart rate settled, too.

But that was too close. He had to get off the side of this damn boat.

He couldn't risk shimmying along the windowsill back to the bow deck. The crew members were still in the passageway. The risk that he would be seen was too great. And he wasn't at all sure he could navigate the return journey without slipping and falling into the sea. But he couldn't cling to the side of the ship until they were gone, either. His arms were already tired, his hands already cramping. He'd be shark bait inside of ten minutes.

That left only one option. He had to get to the aft deck.

Where Paloma and Stratham were talking. And where the Whitley and her crew were headed.

Paul had a tenuous grip on the rim of the superstructure where it angled down toward the deck rail. If he could swing along that rim, monkey-bar style, he could make it to the rail.

But then he'd be even more exposed. The top of the rail was made of curved gold, but the wall of the rail was clear glass. He'd be hanging there in plain sight of anyone on the deck.

He reset his hands and feet, pressed his hips forward against the side of the yacht for stability, and arched his head back, trying to get a better view of what lay before him.

He could see the angle of the superstructure, could see the glass wall of the rail, could see Paloma and Stratham sitting across from each other at the table. Stratham's back was toward Paul.

Across from him, the glow of the firepit lit Paloma's face. Under other circumstances, Paul might have wanted to take a moment to appreciate the beauty of the scene. Instead, he pressed himself back against the ship so Paloma wouldn't look up and see him.

His heart hammered again, but not from fear this time. Paul had seen another possibility.

He craned his head up. A faint white glow edged the gumdrop shapes of the GPS array in faint silver against the dark sky.

The helipad was directly above him.

There was no way for him to climb up there directly. No safe way, at least. No sane way. But the spiral stairwell that led to the helipad was just to his right, just inside the aft deck. If he could shimmy a few feet to his side and climb over the rail, he might be able to sneak around to the front of the stairs and up to the helipad without being seen. Once there, he could wait as long as necessary for everyone else to go away.

Again, it wasn't a great option, but it was a hell of a lot better than hanging off the side of a yacht at sea.

Paul pressed his body flat against the aluminum superstructure, feeling the cold seep through the thin white dress shirt into his chest, through the tuxedo pants into his thighs and knees. He closed his eyes and focused on his breath, breathing in, holding, breathing out, holding. He slowed his breaths, slowed his heart rate, focused on each section of his body—feet, legs, belly, arms, chest, neck—and visualized the muscles loosening with each outbreath.

Once relaxed and focused, he tested his grip with his left hand and his foothold with his left foot, gripped hard, and shifted his right hand further out. With his right hand set, he took another deep, rhythmic breath.

If he was going to fall to his death in the cold, night sea, this was when it would happen.

He let that thought drift through his mind, then pushed it away and focused on the next movement.

In one smooth motion, he pushed off as best he could with his left foot and swung himself to the right, holding on by only his right hand against the rim of the angled superstructure.

His right hand had started to sweat. Pulled now by the weight of his entire body, it slipped, his skin screeching along the metal rim like nails on a chalkboard. Panic leapt into Paul's throat again. Again his cowardly heart tried to abandon his body to save itself.

Paul flung his left arm out in desperation, caught the rim of the superstructure just enough to curl the first knuckle of his left hand over it. His body banged against the side of the ship, his shoes thumping against the metal.

He scrabbled his feet against the superstructure, pressed with his knees, bucked with his hips, tugged with his fingertips and managed to squirm up the side of the ship and get a more secure grip with both hands.

He hung there for a long time, eyes closed, feeling the cold metal now cooling the panicked sweat from his body. Once the pounding in his ears subsided, he listened closely for any voices, any alarms from the deck above him. His shoes had made a racket against the side of the ship, and Paul had no idea how well that could be heard inside.

After what felt like an eternity, when his heart rate had finally slowed again, when no shouting came from above, when no one dragged him up over the rail or pushed him down into the sea, Paul reset his grip, dried the sweat from first one hand, then the other, on his pant legs, and started again.

It was easier now that he'd made the jump from the windowsill to the rail, but no less dangerous. He had nowhere for his feet to rest. His entire weight was supported by his hands, and they held on by a knuckle and a half of each finger.

And, even through the adrenaline, Paul could feel the soreness in his hands and arms. He was a thief, not a bodybuilder, and he'd already been clinging to the outside of the ship for at least five or ten minutes. His muscles wouldn't hold out forever.

He swung his legs back and forth in small arcs like the pendulum of a grandfather clock, working up a rhythm, gaining momentum that he hoped would help him move along the lip of the superstructure. Once he'd gotten the rhythm going, he worked his hands. Swing out, shift the right hand, swing back. Swing out, shift the left hand, swing back. Again and again he used this rhythm to work himself across the rail, six inches at a time. He didn't dare reach further for fear he'd overextend himself and fall.

He only had to go ten feet, but it felt like a mile. He worked slowly, methodically until his right hand found the top of the rail, where he could get a full grip. That made things less difficult, but they became more dangerous. Once he got his left hand on the rail beside his right, he'd be exposed through the glass to anyone who looked in his direction. He would have to move quickly to avoid that risk.

He took another deep breath and swung his left hand over. His face pressed against the glass wall. Through it, he could clearly see Paloma and Stratham sitting at the table. Stratham's back was still to Paul, but Paloma faced him directly. At the moment, her head was turned, talking to the first officer, who stood beside the table. Paul couldn't see the two crew members, but he assumed they were still in the bedroom, checking for evidence they could destroy.

They were all distracted for the moment, but if any of them glanced over at him while he came over the rail, he'd be caught. He had to be quick and quiet, two things he wasn't sure he could manage with arms burning and half-numb from hanging off the side of the yacht for what felt like forever.

But there was no time to complain, and no time to plan. He had to move.

He swung his legs in that pendulum motion again, thankful that his pants and shoes were black and unobtrusive in the night. When he had some momentum, he swung his legs hard to the left and levered himself up with his arms, struggling against the side of the rail with his thighs, careful to keep his feet lifted well away from anything that could make noise if he bumped them. All the time, as he grunted softly and worked his way up, his arms quivering, he kept his eyes focused on the table, watching for any sign that he had been heard or seen. Fortunately, Paloma and the first officer seemed very intent on their conversation, and Stratham, his back to Paul, didn't look around.

Paul pulled himself up just to the point before he could hook his arms over the rail, kicked with his feet against the air like a caught fish flopping and gasping for air on the deck, trying to gain that last inch.

Finally, he did. He hooked his arm over, socked the top of the rail securely under his armpit, and pulled himself up and over the rest of the way, being sure to land with his feet soft on the deck.

Paul crouched low, behind the spiral stairs leading up to the helipad, watching Paloma and the others through the treads. They didn't look up, showed no sign that they'd noticed him.

His shoulders relaxed. He didn't realize he'd been holding his breath until he let it out in a long, slow movement.

Seizing the opportunity while the others were still distracted, Paul darted around the back of the stair to the opening and climbed the first few steps. They curled around to face the bedroom.

And Paul stopped dead.

Directly in front of him, their head even with his shins, was one of the crew members. He'd just stepped out of the bedroom. His head was down, a cleaning rag in one hand, as he studied the deck and the rail.

He didn't seem to have noticed Paul. But if the crew member looked up, Paul would be discovered.

And if Paloma, Stratham, or the first officer looked over, they would see Paul in plain view on the stairs.

Paul held his breath again, conscious of it this time, doing his best to relax his muscles so he wouldn't make a sound. He heard his heart beating in his ears, the pulse getting quicker and quicker.

The crew member ran his rag over the rail that Paul had just climbed, wiping it clean. He peered intently at the rail, at the glass, at the deck beneath it. Probably looking for blood, just as Paul had been doing earlier.

The crew member set one hand absent-mindedly on the side of the stair. If he moved it two inches further in, he'd be touching the toe of Paul's tuxedo shoe. If he looked up, he'd be staring into Paul's eyes in the dark.

He did neither.

He walked around the stair, studying the floor the whole time, and moved off toward the other side of the deck.

Not giving himself time to think, to react, to even let the pounding of his heart slow, Paul took the remaining steps two at a time, soft on the balls of his feet, until he was safely out of sight on the helipad.

When he reached the top, Paul heaved a sigh of relief. The tension immediately drained from him, his heart rate slowing, his breathing moderating.

But when he looked up and saw all the blood, he nearly fell back down the stairs.

21

THE HELIPAD WAS SMALLER than Paul expected. It wasn't much bigger than the diameter of a helicopter's rotors. To land on a pad that small while it was bobbing up and down and left and right on the waves in the ocean, Minsk's pilot had to be an ace.

But there was no helicopter there at the moment. Instead, there was a whole lot of blood.

Minsk's blood, Paul assumed.

It dripped and pooled in a staggered trail from the stairs toward the darkness in the back of the helipad, illuminated by the overspill of the white lights surrounding the circular concrete pad. The thin trail thickened as it moved away from Paul, pooling into thick blood spatters that glinted like quicksilver in the distance.

One foot on the helipad, frozen in shock on the top stair, Paul looked down between his feet and saw the faint shadow of blood spots on the step beneath him. He hadn't noticed in the dark and in his rush to get out of sight.

He glanced over his shoulder and down at Paloma and the others, now smaller and foreshortened from his higher vantage point. They still hadn't noticed him, but they would if he didn't move. There was no direct light on him, but they would see his silhouette against the helipad glow.

Paul stepped up onto the helipad. The wind immediately caught him in the chest, threatened to knock him off balance, knock him back down the stairs or over the side. At this height, with nothing but the GPS array to block it, the wind was a force, like the hand of God pushing Paul wherever it wanted. When the wind gusted, Paul felt like he needed superhuman strength just to stay standing, let alone to move forward. No wonder Minsk felt like a superman up there.

Along the circumference of the pad, white lights set into the concrete pointed straight up into the night sky. They were faint and soft, but when a helicopter was on approach, Paul figured they could probably be brightened to paint a more visible target for the pilot.

As it was, the faint light cast as many shadows as it dispelled. Between the blood splatters and the gloomy lighting, Paul felt like he was walking through a horror scene.

And he supposed he was. Minsk may have been killed up here. Or, at least, the death blows may have been dealt up here. Had to have been. With no blood anywhere down below and so much up here, this must have been where it had all happened.

Paul traced along the blood trail. The line was thin and spotty at first, like drips from Minsk's hand or his forehead, perhaps. As he followed them through the center of the helipad, he came upon a larger splatter, then a thick pool of blood. This must have been where Minsk had been stabbed or shot in the chest. There was too much blood for it to have come from just his head wound.

But there was too much blood, period. The pool was at least three feet wide and thick enough that if Paul had stuck his finger into it, the blood would have come up over his fingernail. There was no way Minsk could have lost that much blood and still been able to climb down a spiral staircase, and walked the length of the entire deck onto the bow deck. Let alone stop for a drink along the way.

Of course, if he had, he'd be pretty out of it from the blood loss. Could explain his erratic behavior on the deck. Maybe the poison wasn't the culprit. Maybe the residue wasn't from poison at all.

No, it had to be. The chemical taste, the cloudy residue. Something was added to Minsk's vodka. It may not have killed him, but something was going on there.

Paul frowned down at the pool of blood. Then he noticed another trail leading away from it. But this trail didn't lead in the direction Paul had come. Not back toward the stairs. This trail led forward, into the gloom cast by the white lights along the edge of the helipad. The darkness hung between the glare of the lights like a shadowy ghost, like a hallucination.

Paul stepped along the blood trail, stopped at the edge of the pad. He held his hands up, forming blinkers around his eyes, letting them adjust to the gloom in front of him, to chase away the ghost.

When his eyes finally adjusted, Paul jumped back, nearly slipped in the pool of blood.

He'd seen a body.

A dead body.

Hidden in the gloom.

Paul's mind raced as fast as his heart, scrambling for explanations even as his vital signs went crazy. Was this where the crew had dragged Minsk's body? Seemed like a dumb place to put it.

When his heart rate had settled from the shock, Paul stepped forward again. He pulled his phone from his jacket and turned on the flashlight. It did little to dissipate the gloom, but it cast enough light for Paul to make out the corpse's features, if he leaned close enough.

The corpse was a woman. Maybe mid-thirties. Paul's age, or

a little older. She wore a white shirt and black necktie over black pants, a black apron tied around the waist. A server's outfit. Whoever it was, this person was working as a server for the party.

Or masquerading as one.

Paul crept closer.

The woman's hair was pulled tight into a pony tail on the back of her head. Paul swallowed hard even as his mouth went bone dry. He shined his flashlight closer on the woman's hair.

White-blond hair with a single streak of pink.

This was the server Paul had followed up the stairs earlier in the evening.

Her face looked Slavic, with a long, angular nose and a narrow mouth. Pretty. Her brown eyes were open, staring up into the night sky. With his foot, Paul turned her to one side.

He finally found where all the blood had come from. The back of the woman's shirt was soaked in it. Paul bent down and shined his light closer, holding the woman on her side with his fist, careful not to leave any fingerprints.

The white shirt was ripped in at least a dozen places. Thin slits torn in the fabric.

Knife wounds.

This woman had been stabbed to death. Stabbed many, many times.

He eased her body flat on the helipad again, looked more closely at her face. No signs of bruising on her cheeks or her neck, but her collar was soaked dark red with blood. Paul found a deep wound dug into her neck toward the back. That was probably the killing blow, a deep jab from behind, into her jugular.

Had it been Minsk? Why would Minsk want to kill a random server at his party?

Maybe she wasn't a server. Minsk was into some shady business. Shady business meant shady business partners. The woman looked like she could be Russian. Maybe she'd been hired to kill Minsk. She'd come to the party, posed as a server, lured Minsk onto the helipad somehow and tried to assassinate him. Maybe she'd been hired by a rival arms dealer or a drug lord that Minsk had rubbed the wrong way. Probably an occupational hazard in the circles Minsk had traveled. He probably fended off an assassination attempt every other week.

If she'd actually slipped through posing as a server, Minsk's fabled security staff must be shit. That would explain how Paul had gotten on the yacht so easily. Guess money can't buy everything after all.

With this new theory, Paul figured the assassin had found Minsk on the helipad and attacked him. Despite the surprise, Minsk had gotten the upper hand. They struggled, Minsk stabbed the woman repeatedly in the back, then delivered the blow to the neck. Once she was dead, Minsk dragged her off to the side of the helipad, probably intending for his men to dispose of the body later, and walked toward the stairs. The blood spatter had come from the knife in Minsk's hand. Maybe he'd wiped it clean and put it back in his pocket. Maybe he'd thrown it into the sea from the stairs.

But Minsk had been injured, too, a nasty cut to his head and a deadly wound to his chest. Could be the assassin was good, had slipped by Minsk's security through her own skill rather than the incompetence of the security team. Maybe she'd managed to shoot Minsk in the chest before he got the better of her. From this height, the wind would carry the sound of the gunshot away, alerting no one. Or maybe she'd had a knife and stabbed him in the heart, cut him across the forehead during their struggle.

Paul swore under his breath, the soft sound silenced by the wind whipping by. He was just inventing stories now. He had no idea what was really going on. He wished he'd been more aware, had taken more time in the moment to notice Minsk's wounds.

Had the head wound been thin, like a knife cut, or ragged and bruised, like blunt force trauma? Had the blood on his shirt been from a knife wound or a gunshot?

The only way to know would be to find Minsk's body again and study it. The body had to be somewhere. It was a yacht, after all. Only so many places to stash a corpse.

The helipad was not one that Paul would have thought of. He looked more closely at the wound on the dead woman's neck. It was deep, almost all the way through. Paul could see a small nick in the front where the tip of the knife had emerged. The length of the slit was about two inches. Could have been a switchblade or some other kind of knife Minsk carried on his person. The wound was wider at one end than the other. Minsk had jammed the knife into the woman's neck, then twisted it for good measure.

Paul checked the woman's pockets, checked her apron, looking for identification or weapons of any kind. He found nothing. If she'd had a gun or a knife, Minsk had either taken it or thrown it overboard.

The dead assassin would explain Minsk's chest wound and the head wound, but the poison was still a mystery. Maybe the assassin delivered the poison, too. Maybe she'd followed Minsk to the helipad, brought him a glass of vodka laced with poison. Then he'd figured out who she was and killed her, but the assassin had already delivered a killing blow to the chest, and Minsk drank the vodka after the fight.

Paul shook his head. It was too ridiculous to make sense. Even if it were true, the vodka would have spilled in the fight. And even if it hadn't, why the hell would Minsk drink from a glass brought to him by an assassin?

For that matter, what the hell were they doing on the helipad in the first place? Had Minsk gone up there for a super stroll? Paul had seen Paloma silhouetted in the window. Minsk had approached her and she'd turned away. Had they quarreled?

Had Minsk gone to the helipad to calm himself with a walk? Could Paloma have poisoned him after they fought?

Paul crossed the pad again, poked his head carefully over the edge, looking down on the deck below. Paloma and Stratham were gone. The two crew members were talking with First Officer Whitley, who pointed them into the bedroom, then checked around the deck. Paul ducked back out of sight just as she turned around.

They'd finished the deck and headed back inside to continue their cleaning. They'd already come down the passageway on the left side of the ship, the port side, so odds were they'd continue down the starboard side to the dressing room, the bathroom, the office. Paul could probably slip away once they'd finished the bathroom.

He sat down on the edge of the helipad to wait. He tried not to think about the corpse laying behind him, the blood splattered across the concrete.

He didn't succeed.

The wind gusted again. Paul shivered and pulled his tuxedo jacket tight around him, urging the cleaning crew to hurry.

22

PAUL HAD WAITED another fifteen minutes, then crept down the stairs into the bedroom. He spied the crew members in the office, Whitley supervising from the doorway, so he circled around, down the port passageway, through the lounge, and down the stairs. Hopefully without being seen.

Now he was mingling with the crowds outside on the main deck. With the starry sky, the cool breeze, and the expensive champagne, it was a beautiful party, despite the bland jazz and the even blander guests. But Paul couldn't enjoy it. Even while the crowd chittered around him, his mind was still up on the helipad, still back on the owner's deck.

If an assassin had killed Minsk, it seemed strange that Paloma and the captain would cover it up. It was possible they were just trying not to distract from the fundraiser, trying to extract maximum funds from the guests before dealing with Minsk's murder. But then why would they try to pin Minsk's death on Paul? They already had a dead body on the helipad, one that would connect to some organized crime syndicate somewhere in the world. That was an easy enough explanation. Why go to all the trouble to intimidate Paul, some random guest they'd never even seen before?

"About time you showed up."

The voice drifted into Paul's mind, twined with the thoughts spinning there. Paul frowned at the intrusion, trying to fit the new thought in with the others.

"Now you're ignoring me? You really know how to show a lady a good time."

Paul glanced up, his vision clouded by his thoughts, and saw Melantha, octagonal-cut tumbler still in her hand, still wrapped with a napkin, now soaked again. Her arms were folded and she stared at Paul with her eyebrows raised, an amused smile on her lips.

Her lips may have been smiling, but the annoyance was very clear in her eyes.

"Sorry," said Paul. "Sorry, I was just—"

"If you say preoccupied, I'm going to go sit with that guy over there." She pointed to a white-haired man hunched at a table in the corner, staring dumbly at his drink. He had to have been at least ninety years old, and it didn't seem like his mind was running at full capacity anymore. "He'll be more interesting to talk to, I'm sure."

Paul stared at the tumbler in her hand. His mind flashed back to Minsk sitting on the deck by the hot tub, sitting like a stone carving, sweat from the glass dripping over his hand. Then Minsk crushing Paul's wrist in an iron grip, that wildness in his eyes—

"Hey." Melantha's touch on his shoulder shook Paul from his memory. "Are you okay?"

Paul startled away from her. She held up both hands, placating.

His eyes focused on her face. Where before he'd seen annoyance, now he saw concern. Shame flooded over him. Paul glanced around at the guests nearby. None of them seemed to have noticed. They continued dancing badly and talking too loud.

He smiled weakly at Melantha and ran a hand over his forehead, surprised when it came back slick with sweat.

"Sorry," he said.

"That's your favorite word these days."

Again, he attempted a smile. The pitying look on Melantha's face told him he'd failed.

"Okay, come with me," she said, wrapping an arm around Paul's shoulder and leading him toward the back of the deck. "That old man's giving me the stalker eyes. I don't want to have to break his heart."

Paul looked over his shoulder. The old man was still staring hunch-shouldered at his drink.

Melantha led Paul down a set of stairs into a room underneath the deck they'd just been standing on. An indoor pool filled nearly the entire space, the floor of the deck above forming a low ceiling. Ripples from the water's undulating surface reflected on it, the underwater lighting casting wild, kaleidoscopic shapes across the walls and ceiling. The glow of the lights in the pool was the only illumination, giving the space a dreamy feeling, like they were already underwater.

A yacht with an indoor pool. Though he'd seen it on his tour with the captain, Paul still shook his head. Unbelievable.

There wasn't much seating save for one soft bench in the corner, not much to do in the room but swim. As a result, the room was empty. No guests. Paul could still hear the occasional riffle of fake laughter, the occasional clomp of a heavy dance step above them. Otherwise, the room was silent save for the soft lapping of the pool water and the quiet hum of the yacht machinery.

Paul thought back to the deck map in his mind. He remembered seeing this space on the map, but hadn't realized it was an indoor pool. They had to be close to the engine room, just one or two decks below them.

Melantha stepped behind a bar at the far end of the pool,

opened a mirrored cabinet door, and took a bottle down from a high shelf. She dropped a single, large square of ice in a tumbler —a smooth-sided tumbler, Paul noticed—and poured a healthy measure of whiskey from the bottle.

"You look like you need this," she said, holding the glass out to Paul.

Paul took it and pulled down a long sip. It tasted every bit as good as what Paloma had served him earlier.

Melantha watched him closely as he drank. Seeing his reaction, she nodded, seemingly satisfied, topped off his drink, and put the bottle back where she'd found it. She stepped around the bar and waved for Paul to follow her through a side door, down a short passageway, and into a small room with a short couch and a coffee table sat in front of a wide window looking out at the surface of the water. A gas fireplace hung embedded in the wall, low flames dancing over blue glass stones, mingling its soft light with the even softer lighting overhead.

She set her drink on the table and sat on the couch, patted the cushion beside her. A command, not a suggestion. Paul did as he was told.

Melantha settled into the couch, crossed her legs at the knee. The couch was wide enough for three people, but they sat close enough that, as she crossed her legs and the golden satin of her dress slid softly away, the full length of her bare thigh pressed against the side of Paul's pant leg.

Heat flowed into his body. Paul wasn't sure if it was coming from the fire or from Melantha. But her thigh was no longer the only thing pressing against Paul's pants.

They sat on the couch for a long moment, enjoying the quiet, enjoying the view. The dark surface of the sea sat only a few feet below the windows, lit by the glow from the decks above, reflected on the gentle lines of the yacht's wake. The waves and the movement broke the reflection of the party into shifting swirls of light and shadow, suggesting the party above, but never giving Paul a clear view of it.

In the distance, a thin line on the horizon, Paul could see the shore, far enough away that it seemed like a different world. He remembered coming through this deck earlier with the captain, but the captain hadn't shown him the indoor pool, hadn't pointed out this small lounge. Paul wondered what else the captain hadn't shown him.

And he wondered how Melantha knew so much about the yacht, how she seemed so comfortable stepping behind someone else's bar and pouring a drink. Paul didn't think he would do that at someone else's party. Her casual knowledge of the nooks and crannies and secret spots suggested this wasn't the first time she'd been there.

Then again, he was the one who had slipped away at his first opportunity and wandered the yacht alone, peering behind every door and through every window.

Paul took a sip of his drink then leaned forward and set it on the coffee table beside Melantha's, the octagonal-cut tumbler with the soaked cocktail napkin stuck to the sides. She carried it around with her like a security blanket.

"You ex gave you that drink?" Paul said, nodding toward the tumbler.

Melantha glanced at it. "Yeah, why?"

"Where is he now? Or she?"

"*He* is around somewhere, I'm sure. I haven't seen him for a while."

"You guys aren't close?"

"That's what ex means, doesn't it?"

Paul shrugged. "He invited you to the party."

She picked up her drink, raised it to her lips. "I never said he invited me." She watched him over the rim of the glass as she drank.

Paul watched her back. Something about her stare, her

entire presence, excited Paul—the tightness in his pants was evidence of that—but unsettled him, too. Maybe it was her forwardness. Maybe it was her beauty. Maybe Paul just wasn't used to being pursued so boldly. Melantha made him nervous, but in a good way. He thought.

He picked up his own drink and took a sip, more for something to do under her gaze than because he wanted it. Amusement flashed through her dark eyes. She seemed to know the effect she had on him. Seemed to enjoy his disquiet. She set her tumbler back on the table.

"Feeling good?" she asked, gesturing toward Paul's drink.

Paul looked down at the whiskey, swirled it in the glass. The huge cube of ice nearly touched the sides of the glass, knocked softly against it as he swirled.

"Yes," he said, and, despite the disquiet in his mind, he meant it. There was nothing like a beautiful woman to take your mind off your problems. "I am. Thank you."

Even while she made his heart beat erratically, made his mind spin in circles, something about Melantha did set Paul at ease. There was an electricity that crackled between them, sparks that set Paul's hair standing on end. But there was something about her energy that calmed him, too. The calm strength in her stare, maybe. The smooth, sultry sound of her voice.

It certainly wasn't the voluptuous curves of her body. He eyed the line of her thigh against his leg. Those curves didn't calm Paul one bit.

And Melantha seemed to know it. She plucked the drink from his hand, leaned forward to set it on the table, then leaned back and slowly, ever so slowly, uncrossed her legs and crossed them again, this time with the other leg on top. The slit in her dress, pushed back and held by the couch cushion, offered Paul a full view of the process.

The straps of her heels twined back and forth up the slow curve of her calves. Her full, smooth thighs parted for a tantalizing moment, then closed again as the other leg came over. Paul had the briefest glimpse between them—though he may have been imagining it. His imagination was working overtime in that moment. It seemed the smooth satin of Melantha's dress may have been the only thing touching her skin, anywhere on her body.

In that moment, Paul wanted to add one more thing to that list.

Melantha smiled, a slow smile that parted her lips like she'd parted her thighs, as she watched Paul watch her. She set one long arm on the back of the couch, teased Paul's neck with her fingers, sending shivers through his body.

"I'm glad you're feeling good," she said, her voice a husky whisper that sent a whole new set of shivers racing through Paul's body. She slid her hand into his hair, around the back of his head, turned his head toward her. He stared into her deep, dark eyes. Slid his gaze down to her lips. Her dark red lipstick beckoned him. He wanted nothing more than to answer. Her smile spread them again, slow and sultry, spread red lips over perfect, white teeth.

Then those teeth parted as she gripped him behind his head, pulled him slowly toward her.

"I'm going to make you feel even better," she whispered as she slid her bare leg over him, straddled his lap, pulled his lips to hers.

And she did.

Oh, did she ever.

23

PAUL DIDN'T KNOW what time it was. Didn't care.

He didn't know how long he and Melantha had been below deck. He didn't care.

But as he stood amidst the partygoers again, back on the main deck with the starry sky, the cool breeze, the bland jazz, he felt like he had just woken from a dream. Or fallen back into one.

If not for the drink in his hand, the single cube of ice now melted, curved around the edges and sagging in the center, he wouldn't have believed what had just happened, would have thought he'd hallucinated the entire thing.

But he hadn't. The drink in his hand was proof. He took a pull, just to be sure it, too, was real. It tasted more watery than before, but just as good.

Melantha had disappeared. Off somewhere to powder her nose, she'd said.

Paul stood in the center of the same crowd of bland people, but somehow the lights seemed warmer, brighter. The laughter seemed more convivial, less fake. The dancing was just as cringe-worthy, but that fact seemed less damning, more amusing than before.

Paul shook his head. He was a man, more than thirty years old, and sex with a beautiful woman still left him as giddy as his first time. He wasn't sure what that said about him, whether it made him seem charmingly boyish or hopelessly naive. But in that moment, he didn't care. He just basked in the afterglow.

He took another sip of his drink, scanning the crowd, riding the benevolence in his heart. A movement drew his eye up, up to the rail two decks above. Paloma stood there. She caught his gaze. A quick smile dissolved into a puzzled expression.

She was probably wondering why Paul looked so stupidly happy.

If his expression matched his feelings, in the next moment his face would have looked just as puzzled as Paloma's. Because in that moment, someone came up beside Paloma at the rail.

Melantha.

They conferred briefly, then looked down at Paul together. Stunned, he didn't do anything. No wave or smile or scowl. Just slack-jawed confusion on his face, he was sure. He didn't know that Melantha and Paloma knew each other, let alone knew each other well enough for Melantha to walk onto Paloma's private deck and speak with her alone. Their body language suggested that they were close, comfortable with each other. There was none of the well-practiced formality that Paloma had first had with Paul.

Paloma nodded to Melantha and Melantha backed away, standing well behind the rail. She was still visible in the shadows, but didn't distract from Paloma's presence. She didn't look at Paul.

"Ladies and gentlemen," Paloma called. As if on cue, the jazz music faded to silence. The crowd stopped dancing and mingling. The chatter stopped, and all eyes raised to the woman at the rail.

Paloma surveyed them quietly for a moment. Her command of the audience was absolute, and she knew it. She held them all gently in the palm of her hand, held them in a subtle moment of silence to be sure they could feel her power. Her beauty, her regal posture, her confidence radiated from her. If that weren't enough to command attention, knowledge of her wealth did the rest of the work.

"I hope you've enjoyed the party," she said. There were murmurs of assent throughout the crowd, a few half-empty glasses of champagne lifted toward her in affirmation. Paloma smiled in response, dazzling the crowd even more with her radiance. She really was a force of nature, much more than her husband had ever been. Where he led with fear, Paloma inspired undying love and adoration. A far more powerful motivator.

"The party's not over quite yet, but as we turn back toward shore, I want to remind you of why we're all here: to support Attorney General William Jenkins in his bid for the presidency of the United States." She let her voice rise in a triumphant crescendo. The applause from the crowd was polite, but full. Not just a smattering here and there. The guests were people who really seemed to believe in the AG.

"Now I know, I know," smiled Paloma. "He hasn't formally announced his candidacy. Yet." She winked at them all, an intimate gesture that she somehow managed to translate to the crowd while standing twenty feet above them and thirty feet away. The crowd laughed. "But our show of support tonight will do wonders for inspiring in our Attorney General the confidence that he really can make a difference, even more than he already has." A smattering of applause. "He's already pursued drug lords and arms dealers, making our world infinitely safer for us and our children and grandchildren."

The crowd cheered. Ironic, given that their host—their late host—had probably ratted out his own colleagues in exchange for immunity and favors from the government to enrich his own arms dealings.

"He has put countless criminals behind bars, including Russian spies, domestic terrorists, and the most notorious serial killer the world has ever seen."

More cheers and applause. And Paul was sure, again, that those Russian spies had been friends of Minsk's at one point. They probably pissed him off somehow, so he railroaded them. Jenkins would have been only too happy to chase down Minsk's tips to make himself look better.

"He has even rooted out corruption in the highest levels of our own government," Paloma continued, "putting three U.S. Congressmen and a Supreme Court justice behind bars."

Again, applause from the crowd, though with fewer cheers than before. Some of the guests probably lost money on those convictions. Their own contributions to the congressmen involved had probably been greasing those corrupt wheels for who knows how long.

"When Attorney General William Jenkins becomes President William Jenkins, how much more good will he do?" A cheer. "How much safer will America be?" Cheer. "How much more prosperous will all of us become?"

A big cheer for that line, with Paloma herself pumping her fists and clapping and smiling with the crowd. Paloma had used the word "us". Ostensibly, she meant all of America. But, really, she meant people like the guests clapping and cheering around Paul. There's nothing the wealthy like more than the promise of a future where they become even wealthier.

"But as you well know, political campaigns don't run on goodwill alone." The crowd groaned theatrically, fully into it now. Paloma was pulling them in like a carny at a shooting gallery. Twenty shots for a dollar. Step right up. Just one hit wins the prize. "Campaigns are expensive, and they need donations from good people, patriotic people, true Americans like all of you. Generous donations, to bring about the kind of change, the kind of progress this country needs to continue to be the best country in the world. To be the America we love."

Big cheers from the crowd.

"And your contributions tonight have been most generous. You truly are good, patriotic Americans. I'm sorry that the Attorney General could not be here to thank you in person tonight. And I'm sorry my husband's illness prevents him from standing here beside me."

Minsk's illness was a bad one, indeed. Incurable. A terminal case of murder.

"But, on behalf of both of them, on behalf of America, and on behalf of myself, an immigrant who became a citizen when she realized the majesty and glory and infinite opportunity this country affords to those who have the passion, the will, and the talent to work for it, I thank you." She clasped her hands together in front of her face, as if in prayer. "Deeply, truly, I thank you."

Sustained applause, then. Paul corrected himself. The only thing the wealthy like more than the promise of more prosperity for themselves is the acknowledgement that the prosperity they have now was earned by the sweat of their brow and their own God-given talent. Definitely not from pure good luck and the lottery of birthright. They like to be told that the superiority they claim is actually justified.

"So please," Paloma said, "enjoy the rest of the party. But, as you do, as you drink the fine champagne and eat the delicious food and admire the beautiful view, remember what makes it all possible. Your generosity is what protects the freedoms that make America strong."

Paloma waved goodbye from the deck above. The crowd applauded, then turned back to chattering and mingling as the music faded in again. A few in the crowd went back to dancing. Others moved toward the salon, or turned in earnest back to their schmoozing and networking.

She'd pulled them in like a carny, charmed them like a carny, pulled their money from their wallets in front of their own eyes, just like a carny.

But at the carnival, the game is rigged.

Paul knocked back the rest of his drink, set the empty glass on a side table, and slipped through the crowd into the salon. The afterglow was gone. Melantha and Paloma were upstairs together, and Paul wanted to know why.

24

PAUL STOOD outside the sliding door that led to Paloma's salon, hoping to overhear what Paloma and Melantha were saying inside. Unfortunately, the construction on the yacht was too good. The doors were well made and practically soundproof. He couldn't hear anything.

Except the sound of someone clearing their throat behind him.

He turned and saw Vernon Stratham pushing his glasses up his nose and rocking back and forth on both heels.

"Is there something I can help you with, Mr. Baker?" he asked.

Paul glanced down at the laptop Stratham clutched in both hands. It would sure help if Stratham let Paul have a look at the laptop for a few minutes. But he supposed that suggestion wouldn't be very well-received. That idea fell more into the "beg forgiveness" category than the "ask permission" one.

"Not at all, Mr. Stratham. I was just going inside to congratulate Mrs. Minsk on her speech."

"It was an effective one," he said. "Just in making my way up here, I've been approached by several guests inquiring about increasing their donations." He patted the laptop with one hand, rubbed it lovingly. Paul wasn't even sure Stratham was aware of the gesture. It may have been subconscious. Regardless, it only deepened Paul's desire to get inside that computer. If Minsk's system hadn't given him anything, maybe Stratham's would.

"I thought there were caps on campaign donations," said Paul.

"Direct contributions, yes. But," Stratham smiled, "there are many ways to support a candidate."

"Right," said Paul. Stratham's smile was innocent enough, but Paul still felt like he needed a shower. Yet another reminder of why he would never get into politics.

That, and his childhood spent committing felonies with his parents.

After staring uncomfortably at each other for an awkward moment, Stratham gestured toward the sliding door. "Shall we?" he said.

Paul followed him through the doorway.

"Good enough for you, Vern?" said Paloma as she came inside from the deck. The wall was still open, and the air inside the salon was taking a turn toward the chilly side. Paul pulled his tuxedo jacket around his shoulders, wondering how the women could stand to walk around all night in thin dresses that left more skin exposed than covered.

Not that he minded the style. He eyed Melantha as she followed Paloma, enjoying the way the satin fabric of her gown caressed the skin beneath, skin that only a short time ago he had been caressing himself. The memory brought a faint smile to his lips. But when his eyes met Melantha's, there was no smile there. There was no recognition there at all.

"An excellent speech, Mrs. Minsk," said Vernon, nodding as he sat on the long, semicircular couch in the center of the room and set his laptop on the table in front of him.

"At least as good as my husband would have done, no?"

"Probably better," said Vernon as he opened the laptop.

"Good answer, Vern." Paloma smiled back at Melantha. "Maybe men can learn new tricks after all," she said. She flashed a look at Paul as she turned back around. "What did you think, Mr. Baker?"

"Stirring," said Paul, his mood soured by Melantha's look. "As far as political speeches go."

Paloma walked around the couch to stand beside Vernon. "That wasn't a political speech," she said. She put her hand on her chest, her face taking on a pained, serious look. "That speech came from my heart. I'm an immigrant, and America is the shining light on the hill. All of us poor folk who weren't lucky enough to be born here live our entire lives dreaming of the day we can call ourselves American."

A single tear formed in the corner of one of her eyes.

Stratham cleared his throat. "If you don't mind," he said.

Paloma broke into a smug smile. "See, Vern," she said, keeping her eyes on Paul, "I've got these speeches down pat. Hell, I may as well run for office myself."

"I'll be happy to support you, Mrs. Minsk," said Stratham, "but right now, I'd like to review these contribution numbers with you."

She sat down beside him with a sigh. "I've said it before and I'll say it again, Vern. You would never make it as a candidate. You're just not likable enough."

She glanced at Melantha and winked. Melantha's stony expression didn't shift.

"My job does not require me to be liked," Stratham said, then pointed to the laptop screen. "It does require me to be attentive to detail."

They fell into discussion of whatever was on the computer. Paul came around behind the couch to get a better look.

And to stand beside Melantha.

"I didn't know you and Paloma were friends," he said quietly.

On the laptop, Stratham was pointing out various numbers on a spreadsheet.

"You didn't ask," Melantha replied. "And I don't know if I'd call us friends." She tilted her head to one side. "Maybe someday."

"What are you then?"

Melantha considered the question for a moment. "Co-workers," she said. "I suppose."

Paul frowned, nodding as he looked at the laptop screen from behind the couch and over Paloma's shoulder. There were names down one column, dates down another, dollar values down a third, with some other data in other columns after that.

Co-workers? What the hell did that mean?

"What kind of work do you do?" he asked. "I thought you said you were a..." He thought back to earlier that night, but his memory failed him. The last few hours felt like weeks. "What did you say you do for a living?"

"I don't think I did," Melantha replied.

"You don't think you did what?"

"Tell you what I do for a living."

The pause was awkward. "So, what do you do for a living?"

Her stare was stone-hard. "My business."

Gone was the sultry, seductive Melantha. This Melantha was telling Paul in no uncertain terms to keep his nose out of her affairs.

Most men would have been thrilled to have an encounter with a gorgeous woman who expected nothing in return. No strings attached. But Paul felt sick to his stomach. He didn't mind if Melantha wasn't looking for a relationship, if she'd just wanted a quickie for some reason. He just wished he'd known that beforehand. He would have kept his feelings more in check. It would have spared him the disappointment that was gnawing a hole in his chest.

Paul followed Melantha's gaze back to the laptop screen,

pushed his feelings to the side, forced himself to focus on the words and the numbers there. The spreadsheet was a donor list, with each name, the date and amount of their donation, and the entity to which they had donated.

It seemed that Stratham was running the funds through several PACs as well as the Attorney General's actual campaign. Paul assumed he was assigning donations in accordance with campaign finance regulations. Those had become a lot looser in the last ten years or so. Paul saw it in the news every election year. With some Supreme Court ruling a while back, companies like the PACs on Stratham's spreadsheet could spend as much money as they liked on political campaigns, flooding the airwaves and the internet with whatever rhetoric they wanted to put out there to support one candidate or attack another.

Paul had no idea how legal or proper it was for AG Jenkins' campaign finance manager to be managing a bunch of PACs that were supposed to be independent, but he didn't really care. That kind of information wasn't going to help Paul. It seemed that everyone bent the rules these days, even the people who swore to uphold them.

The PACs were named things like Forward For America and Americans for Prosperity and other pseudo-inspiring titles that were euphemisms for greed and maintaining the status quo. Paul wondered if the people naming these things smelled their own bullshit, or if they'd become so used to it that they thought the air smelled that way everywhere.

From behind the couch, he scanned down the list of donor names. He recognized one or two from the news, CEOs and tech founders and media moguls. The occasional movie star or rock star or celebrity chef. The donation numbers were all in the six figures, with some much higher, over a million dollars. Just the thirty or so on the screen added up to a massive amount, and the list seemed to scroll forever.

Stratham pointed to one row on the spreadsheet. "Which one was this, Mel?" he said over his shoulder.

"Angel investor," she replied. "Sold her AI music recommendation service a couple years ago."

"AI tech, music recommendation, angel investor..." Stratham muttered as he typed the information into the document.

Mel? Not Melantha or Ms. Woods? Stratham was so formal with everyone else. He glanced at Melantha, but her expression was as stony as it had been before.

Paul took a step back from the couch, his head suddenly pounding. He needed some distance. He was getting too close, too sucked in to the people. He needed to keep his head clear and sharp. Paloma Minsk was friendly, but she wasn't a friend. She had threatened Paul just a few hours earlier, threatened to turn him into the police, to frame him for a murder he didn't commit. She was only letting him move around because she didn't think he could escape, didn't think he could cause any trouble if he were allowed to roam free on the yacht.

Paloma was the ringleader. She had told the captain what to do about Paul. She was the one that Stratham seemed to report to. Even Melantha seemed to defer to Paloma.

Paul didn't know these people. He had no idea of their history, their relationships to each other. He had no clue what their goals were, their motives, their plans. He'd stepped into their lives, not the other way around.

And now he needed to find a clean way to step out again.

To get what he needed, *then* step out again.

This was just a job. He reminded himself for the millionth time. A job like any other. Paloma had made that job harder, for sure, but it was still just a job. He needed donor information, information that tied Jenkins to Minsk for more than just campaign fundraising. He needed dirt.

No, not just dirt. Mud. Burning hot lava would be even better.

Paul needed something he could use to blackmail the Attorney General of the United States.

The laptop on the table in front of Stratham seemed like the best bet in that moment. But Stratham never let it out of his sight. Never even seemed to put it down. And Paul was sure he'd notice if it went missing, even for a few minutes.

Paul had to think of some way to tap into it without him noticing. He watched Paloma and Stratham confer over the laptop screen. He watched Melantha stare from behind them, her face impassive.

Paul let himself feel the stab of disappointment, of betrayal, of disillusionment, hoping it would clear out of his system. He'd only known her for a few hours and she'd used him for sex. Fine. He didn't realize it at the time and had let himself get a little doe-eyed. Whatever. It happened. To him, it seemed to happen pretty often. But that was on him, not on Melantha.

Now he knew better.

Now he could focus on what he needed to do: get the information he needed about Jenkins.

And figure out who killed Minsk.

25

No one seemed to notice when Paul left Paloma's salon. Not that he could see. When he glanced back over his shoulder as he left the room, Paloma and Stratham were still bent over the laptop screen. Melantha still stood, arms folded and face impassive, behind them.

Good. Paul needed some time to look around, and he didn't want to worry about being followed.

He didn't know what he was looking for. Minsk had been killed by that woman on the helipad, but he'd also been poisoned by someone. Did that matter? He could give Paloma and the captain the story about the assassin, show them her body and the wounds in Minsk's chest and head. That should be enough to get him off the hook.

But who had poisoned Minsk? The question nagged at Paul. He shook his head as he moved away from the door to Paloma's salon. Didn't matter. Focus on the job.

He hadn't yet explored the office on the other side of the stairwell. Stratham had been in there earlier. And there were a few rooms immediately to his left that had been locked earlier. He tried the first one again, pushing the button to open the sliding door.

Paul expected an insistent beep telling him the door was still locked, but instead it opened to a cozy office. Windows lined the far wall. A small desk sat in one corner with a monitor, laptop, and a keyboard on top. A cup full of pens and a pad of paper sat off to one side. Across from the desk, a couch lined one wall, with a soft chair and a low coffee table in front of it. A vase of fresh flowers stood on a side table in the corner beside the door. Paintings hung on the wall, depictions of what looked like rural Europe. Could be Italy or France, but probably Spain, since this was undoubtedly Paloma's office and that's where she was from.

Unlike Minsk's office on the deck above, there was no bar in the room. And unlike Minsk's office, this one had a comfortable feel, a feeling that it had been used, lived in, made comfortable by its owner. The decorative touches with the paintings and the flowers, the dents on the couch and the chair where someone had used them, even the pens on the desk all gave the room a sense of being alive. Minsk's office had seemed more like an elaborate place to store his liquor, cold and uninviting. This had to be Paloma's office. Why there needed to be a second one outside on the same deck, Paul didn't know. Perhaps that one was for visitors and guests, while this was her private space.

Paul sat down at the desk and flipped open the laptop. Unlike Minsk, Paloma was smart enough to have a password on her laptop. Paul considered the effort required to bypass the security and decided he didn't have the time to work on it, not with Paloma right next door and liable to come in at any time. Besides, it didn't seem likely that Paloma's laptop would have any more incriminating information than Stratham's. Stratham's laptop was the gold mine. Paul didn't know why he hadn't thought of it before.

Beside the desk was a small door. Paul went through and found himself in what he assumed was Paloma's bedroom. He was surprised that she would even have a separate bedroom, given the owner's bedroom above. But as he stepped slowly through the room and found Paloma's dressing room, he realized that he'd seen no women's clothes in the dressing room upstairs. It was filled with Minsk's shoes and watches and suits and jeans, but no gowns, no dresses, no women's jewelry.

A glance at the bed—tucked and smoothed, but with skewed pillows, a slight dent in the duvet, a pair of slippers peeking out from under the bed frame—suggested that she had used it recently.

It made sense for Paloma to have her own dressing area, but Paul was surprised they slept apart. Maybe their marriage was in an even worse state than Paul suspected. If Minsk and Paloma slept apart, how separated were the rest of their lives? Could Paloma have poisoned her husband?

"You're not the first man to try to get into my bedroom, Mr. Baker." Paul turned to see Paloma standing in the doorway to the hall. "And you won't be the first one I've kicked out of it, either."

"I'm sorry," Paul stammered, "I—"

Paloma held up one hand. "Please spare us both the boredom of listening to some lame excuse. You got lost? You were looking for the restroom? You were so curious you couldn't help exploring just a little?" She stepped in and took Paul by the elbow, her grip surprisingly firm. And painful. "It may have been charming at first, but it's not anymore."

"Wait, Mrs. Minsk," Paul protested.

Paloma dragged him forward. "The captain really did want to lock you up downstairs," she said.

"Please, just hold on."

"I stopped him before. Don't make me reconsider."

"Paloma, wait." Paul yanked his elbow from her grip. She stopped with an exasperated huff and turned toward him. The flame in her eyes held no amusement this time. It was pure irritation. Hell hath no fury, indeed, and Paul could see in that instant that Paloma Minsk was truly a force of nature. If her husband had gotten on her bad side somehow, he had made a big mistake.

Maybe a deadly one.

"I think I know how your husband was killed," Paul said.

"I think I do, too." Paloma smiled sweetly, then let the smile drop to the floor like a guillotine. "You killed him."

"No," Paul said, "I didn't. But I know who did."

Paloma crossed her arms and stared at Paul, the flames rising in her eyes. Paul had to tread carefully here, he knew.

"Okay, Mr. Baker. Who killed him?"

"An assassin."

She stared at him for a long moment, then grabbed his elbow again. "Fuck the captain. I'm going to lock you up myself."

"No." Paul shook himself free once more, stared hard into the flames that had become an inferno. "I'm serious. And I can prove it."

Paul led a short procession consisting of the captain, Paloma, and First Officer Whitley up the stairwell to the owner's deck, down the passageway through Minsk's bedroom, out the door onto the aft owner's deck, and up the curling staircase toward the helipad. The others followed wordlessly.

Paul told them the story as he led them, assuming that it would be hard to be heard over the wind once they got onto the helipad. He left out the reasons why he'd been on the helipad, left out the sneaking around looking for evidence, the nearly getting caught by Paloma and Whitley, the perilous climb across the outside of the yacht's superstructure. But he told them about the body, about the blood, about the wounds, and about his theory of what happened. They listened without comment.

When Paul got to the top of the stairs and stepped onto the helipad, the wind blasted him. The hand of God once more pushing him back. The captain steadied him with a firm hand on his back, then pushed him forward with enough force to make Paul stumble a step.

The others didn't seem to notice the wind as they stepped onto the helipad, but Paloma hugged herself against the chill. The captain offered his jacket to her and she draped it over her shoulders with a grateful nod.

"This way," said Paul, waving for them to follow. "In the shadows over here."

He hurried across the pad to the spot where he'd seen the assassin's body, gave himself a quick moment for his eyes to adjust. The others crowded in behind him.

"What is it we're supposed to be looking at, Mr. Baker?" asked the captain, his voice that low growl, like a bag of gravel scraping over pavement.

Paul stood silent, dumbfounded.

"Because all I see is a cold owner, an irritated first officer, an idiot guest," he paused for just a moment, looking down at the empty space where the assassin's body should have been, "and the roof of my ship."

26

PAUL COULD NOT BELIEVE what he was seeing.

Or, more to the point, what he wasn't seeing.

"It was here earlier," he stammered. "Right here. A body. A woman."

"A woman's body? Here?" said the captain. "On the roof of the yacht?"

"I know it sounds crazy," said Paul, whirling to face the captain, "but I saw it. It was here."

He looked past the captain toward the center of the helipad. In the soft glow of the landing lights, the helipad surface looked clean and pristine.

"No, no," Paul muttered as he shouldered past the others, strode forward into the center of the pad. "There was blood. A huge pool of it." He got his bearings, then pointed. "Right there. And a blood trail." He walked toward the stairs, pointing at the ground. "Leading back to the stairs."

"Right, right," said the captain. "Mr. Minsk was attacked by the cocktail waitress—sorry, assassin in disguise—and they fought. Right here, you say?"

He pointed to the spot. Paul nodded, his spirits sagging. He knew where this was headed.

"The... assassin... shot Mr. Minsk in the chest, after which he pulled a knife and stabbed her several times in the back before stabbing her again in the neck, killing her. Do I have this right?"

Paul sighed in frustration, the sound lost to the wind gusting across the pad.

"And then he went downstairs—with a bullet still in his chest—made himself a drink, and sat on the deck by the hot tub. He didn't call for help, but instead waited for you to arrive, then attacked you and threw himself over the rail to his death." The captain shrugged. "Makes sense to me."

Paul traced back along the line of the blood trail, back to where he'd seen the pool of blood. Back to where the captain was standing, hands in his pockets. He searched the ground for any trace of blood that the cleaning crew had missed. He found nothing. Just pristine concrete, as clean and clear as the day it had been poured.

"Why would they move it?" he mumbled.

"What was that?" asked the captain.

"Why are you covering this up?" Paul said, loud enough for all three of them to hear him over the wind. "You moved Minsk's body, cleaned everything top to bottom, told the guests he was sick. I get that. He's the owner, the host. You don't want to cause a scene." They stared back at him, all three faces blank, completely inscrutable. "But this woman was just a hired gun. Some mobster's lackey, probably, or a hit man."

"Hit woman," said Paloma with a wry smile.

"She was no one that anyone would notice or care about. Why go to all the trouble of covering up her death?"

"Your theories are very entertaining, Mr. Baker," said Whitley, "but you're pointing out the biggest problem. They just don't make sense."

"Why would my husband kill himself after just escaping murder?" said Paloma.

"Why would he follow a server up to the helipad for a drink?" asked the captain.

"And why would the crew waste our time cleaning up after it all, especially in a place like this where no guest would ever choose to wander?"

"Except for you, of course," said Paloma. "Which raises an interesting question: why did you come up here? In fact, why have you been wandering all over the ship? The captain found you in the engine room. I found you in my bedroom. Now you bring us up here."

"That's a lot of curiosity for a party guest," said Whitley.

"Borders on rude," Paloma said.

"Went past rude a long time ago," growled the captain. "Now it's just suspicious."

Paul could see his mistake now. Those three had no interest in knowing what really happened. And there could only be one reason for that: they already knew.

"I do have one other question," said the captain. Paul looked up at him. "Why did you bring all of us up here? What did you think you would gain?"

"I thought you would see the truth."

"We already know the truth, Mr. Baker," said Paloma. Paul stared at her, startled to have his thoughts echoed so quickly. His surprise turned sour as she met his gaze. A faint smile crossed her lips. It was the smile of a wealthy person, a person with all the power in the world.

"Oh," said the captain, snapping his fingers. "I thought of another question." He looked at Paul. "Do you prefer handcuffs or rope?"

27

PAUL PREFERRED HANDCUFFS. Easier to pick, and he always carried a key in his shoe.

So they tied him with rope.

They locked him on the lowest deck, in a storage room in the stern of the ship. One of the rooms Paul had seen through the porthole window in the door when he'd first stepped onto the yacht and started his self-tour, before he'd run into the captain. The room was close to the engine room. He could hear the clank and whir of the engines through the bulkhead to his left. The sound was loud, even through the wall. The soundproofing on the other decks must have been world class to reduce the engine roar to a just a soft hum up there.

Paul thought back to the deck plans he'd memorized, tried to place himself within the schematic in his mind. He was on the lowest deck, below the waterline. Directly above him would be the indoor pool and the room where he and Melantha had...

Did Melantha know where he was? If so, did she care? She might come looking for him, might set him free. He didn't know why she'd looked at him so coldly in Paloma's salon, especially since her attitude just a few minutes earlier had been anything but cold.

She clearly knew Paloma. She could know about Minsk's death, too. She could be working with Paloma to hide it. That couldn't be true, could it?

Paul shook his head. No. He was done being stupid. His parents had taught him better than that. They'd taught him to think through every situation, to look for angles and opportunities no one else would see because they were too stuck in their own heads, their own worries and ingrained thought patterns.

He had become trapped inside the idea of a beautiful woman falling in love with him, the idea of finding the kind of love his parents had and making the kind of family he had enjoyed for most of his childhood.

Before his father was killed and his mother locked in prison for the rest of her life.

That trap had already snared him too many times. He wasn't going to fall for it again.

And that meant he wasn't going to rely on Melantha anymore. She clearly had some kind of history with Stratham. She clearly already knew Paloma. And she'd lied to Paul about both of those things. Or, at least, hadn't been forthright in revealing them.

But Melantha had only known Paul for a few hours. He couldn't blame her for withholding. Paul was withholding a lot of information from her, too. He tried to use that logic to suppress the bitter betrayal that burned his stomach, the aching disappointment that gnawed his chest. Those feelings were only hurting Paul, distracting him from what he needed to do. And they were coming completely from himself. Melantha had done nothing wrong, aside from the lies. She'd promised Paul nothing, romantically. He'd invented all of the expectations himself.

He shook his head. He was being ridiculous. Tied to a drainpipe in a storage room in the bottom of a megayacht where two murders had already happened and the murderers were still on the loose, and all he could think about was hurt feelings because a woman he'd just met wasn't willing to commit to marriage? Maybe Paul needed to seek psychological help when he got out of this mess.

If he got out of it.

He tested the ropes. Whitley had tied them with the efficiency of a Navy SEAL, like she'd tied hundreds of captives to drainpipes during her career. And for all Paul knew, she had.

But she clearly hadn't tied enough people who already knew how to escape.

The rope was half-inch nylon and looked brand new. They'd had him put his chest against the drainpipe, arms ahead of him, then tied his wrists together so that he was hugging the pipe. Whitley had pulled the ropes tight, tugged them hard enough that, even with the soft nylon, Paul had started to lose feeling in his fingers.

The pipe was metal, painted white. The smell of the new paint was so fresh and strong that Paul could taste it on his tongue, could taste the metal of the pipe. It was smooth enough that he could slide up and down the pipe from the floor to as far as he could reach overhead. That was helpful for his circulation and muscle soreness, but not so helpful for escape. There were no brackets or bolts he could use to cut the rope. Sliding up and down over and over wouldn't generate enough friction because the paint was too slick, too new. And it would have taken forever.

The pipe itself was cool. No heat there. It had to be a drainpipe, not a steam or hot water supply line. That was a good thing, since Paul was snugged up against it, but, again, not so good for getting himself free.

But Paul had already taken care of that. He had pressed his chest tight against the pipe when Whitley tied him, pressed tight and pulled his elbows back, formed his hands into fists and pressed them together at the base of his palms while Whitley tied them with her rope.

As she should have, Whitley had pulled hard with each

wrap of the rope around his wrists, making sure there was no slack. But, while his posture and body language made it look like Paul had given up—and he wore a hangdog expression to sell it even more—his body position was deliberate. By tucking his arms in, making fists, and holding his wrists together, he was making the widest possible diameter for each wind of the nylon rope. No matter how painfully tight Whitley made those winds, she couldn't shrink that diameter.

But Paul could.

Once everyone had left the room, Paul waited for a long time, making sure the others had gone away and forgotten about him, caught up in their other responsibilities. He took that time to acclimate to the sounds and rhythms of the space he was in. The engine sound dominated his hearing, but he eventually was able to tune into other sounds, subtle nuances. The occasional shout let him know the engine crew was still at work, manning and monitoring the engine. The change in rhythm of the engine let him know when the boat was speeding up or slowing down.

He closed his eyes and focused on his body, using his breathing to calm himself, slow his heart rate, and cool his body down from the stress and exertion of being dragged downstairs and tied up. That would also help reduce the diameter of his wrists.

As he focused, he could feel the motion of the ship under his feet, could feel it rise and fall when a particularly large roller came through, could feel when it turned. He figured his bearings and the direction they'd been traveling when they were on the helipad, figured out that a turn to Paul's left was a turn toward shore. They were headed in. Paul was running out of time.

He kept himself calm, though barely. When he was sure no one was coming back and no one was waiting outside the door, when his body had cooled, he set to work.

He pushed his arms forward, extending them as much as he could. He opened his fists and lay his hands flat against each other. If it weren't for the rope and the drainpipe, Paul would have looked in that moment like he was preparing to dive into the ocean.

Instead, he was preparing to escape.

By extending his arms and flattening his hands, he shrank the diameter of the circle around his wrists. Calming himself down and cooling his body temperature diverted blood flow away from his extremities and helped to shrink that diameter even more. Because the rope had been tied when the diameter was larger, all of this created slack. Not a lot, but enough to work with.

He twisted his wrists back and forth, working to stretch the rope and release some of its tension. Nylon rope stretched more when it was new, sometimes adding as much as twenty percent to its length. He moved his arms up and down against each other, pulled his arms back hard against the pole, all the time trying to stretch and loosen the binds.

It hurt. His wrists stung, the skin red and raw and oozing around the rope. And it wasn't quick. Paul wanted to stop a dozen times, to sit down, forget about the ship and the pain and just sleep.

He banged his head against the pipe in frustration, softly at first, then harder and harder as he thought about the blackmail leverage he hadn't found, the detention by the police that would lead to them figuring out and stopping his entire plan. He thought about his mother rotting in prison until the day she died, when she deserved so much better. He banged his head harder and harder.

And then he kept going. He had no other choice. He would rub his wrists to the bone, if that's what it took to free himself, to free his mother.

Progress was slow. It came by the millimeter.

But eventually, after what felt like days but was probably no more than half an hour, it came.

28

PAUL KEPT the rope that had bound him. You never knew when something like that might be useful. He coiled it tightly and shoved it in the outside pocket of his tuxedo jacket.

His wrists felt like fire as he peeked through the porthole window of the door, peeked down both sides of the passageway. It was empty. They'd posted no guard.

Paul didn't know whether to be grateful or insulted.

Before he opened the door, he thought back to the deck plans he'd memorized. If he went left down the hallway, he'd have to go through the engine room again. There was no other way past it. And if the voices he'd heard earlier were really from the engine crew, there would be people in there, people who might have been told to watch for him.

If instead he turned right down the hallway, he could make his way up the ladder and back to the party, rejoin the guests as if nothing had happened, then find a way to slip upstairs. He'd definitely be seen, but only by guests who had no idea what was going on. He could potentially blend in and slip through.

In one direction, he ran the high risk of being caught by two crew members. But if he got past them, there was little chance of being seen by anyone else.

In the other direction, the low risk of being caught by people who would stop him, but the risk never stopped. Paloma, Whitley, the captain, maybe even Stratham or Melantha, they'd all be up there somewhere. And if they caught him again, Paul had no doubt they'd make sure he didn't get free a second time.

Paul crept out the door and turned right. Where he was headed, he would have to deal with Paloma and the others eventually. He'd just as soon not have to deal with the engine crew. He slipped past them once, but he didn't want to push his luck a second time. And if they saw him, even if they didn't stop him, they would alert the captain. Better to blend in than to stand out.

Paul climbed the first ladder he found and emerged into the gym. He remembered it from the deck map and from his tour with the captain. Dumbbells sat in an orderly rack along one wall beside various weight lifting contraptions. A stationary bike with a massive video screen, a high-tech rowing machine with a large cylinder half-full of water on the front, some kind of stair-stepper. All the kind of stuff that Paul never used, had never wanted to use, and would never use.

And he didn't care about it now. But he did care about the water dispenser in the corner and the stack of towels in a rack against the wall. He sucked down some water to ease his thickening tongue and stave off the headache that was already forming after all the whiskey he'd drunk, then wet one of the towels and lay it gingerly over his wrists, hissing as the cold water met his raw, broken skin. He let his wrists soak for a moment, then wiped them clean and dried them on a second towel. Fortunately, the oozing had stopped. He wouldn't have to worry about blood dripping out of his sleeves as he moved through the posh crowd up above.

He folded his cuffs gently over his inflamed wrists. Even the soft fabric of the shirt hurt when it touched the skin. But it offered some protection, both from further injury and from detection. He took his cufflinks from his jacket pocket and fastened the cuffs closed.

Paul poked his head out of the gym. The passageway was empty. He got his bearings and moved quickly and quietly to the stairwell at the center of the ship. He still had two things to do. One was to get Stratham's laptop. The other was to prove that he hadn't killed Minsk.

But to be honest, he didn't give a shit about the second one any more. He had no intention of being on the ship when it docked, so there was no way the police would catch him. And they couldn't interrogate someone who wasn't there. It was clear that someone on the ship had killed the man and was covering it up by moving the bodies. To where, Paul didn't know. He figured, since Whitley and her crew were cleaning everything up, it was probably her and the captain who had done it. He had no idea why.

But the murder didn't matter. Now that he was free again, Paul just needed Stratham's laptop, and then he could get off the damn yacht and end this ridiculous night. In order to do that, he needed to figure out where Stratham was. He was sure the laptop wouldn't be far away.

He climbed the winding stair to Deck Three. Catering staff milled about, rushing back and forth from the salon to the galley and back. After all this time, the guests were still eating and drinking, trying to satisfy their insatiable appetites.

On Deck Four, it was more of the same. Paul could hear the party in the salon as the doors opened and closed. Still going strong. The conversations had grown louder, the awkward laughter a little sharper, more boisterous, more aggressive. Even among the supposedly genteel wealthy folk, alcohol could bring out the worst in them.

Ascending to Deck Five, Paloma's deck, was like walking into a mausoleum. The hush hung heavy on Paul's shoulders. He felt himself instantly tense, on guard for any errant sound or unexpected movement that might come from the captain or Stratham or Paloma herself. Paul had been caught unawares too many times that night. He didn't plan on being caught again.

As he circled the stair, he peered around the landing area. No one there. He dashed up the last few steps two at a time, quiet on the balls of his feet, and slipped into the office. It was the only room he hadn't explored, and it was where Stratham had been when Paul first went into the art gallery.

He closed the door behind him and waited, listening with his ear to the door. He heard nothing but his heart as it slowed from a pound to a thump and then quieted once more.

Paul released a deep breath. He debated for a moment, then pulled the curtain over the window to the office. If someone had been paying attention and had a very good memory, they might have remembered that the curtain had been open. They might wonder why it was closed now. But Paul took the calculated risk that no one paid that much attention to a curtain on a yacht.

He hoped he was right.

The office was much like the others he'd been in, though more impersonal even than Minsk's office. Paneled wood walls. A couch and chairs on one side, a small desk on another, windows along the third. No bar here, which meant that Minsk never used the space. The office was smaller than Paloma's and much smaller than Minsk's, but it was still comfortably roomy.

Paul moved slowly around the room, trying to take every-thing in with soft eyes and an open mind. No expectations, just see what is there.

Unfortunately, he saw nothing.

Nothing on, under, behind, or beside the couch. Nothing on or under the desk. No nooks or corners where Stratham might have put something Paul could use. The room was as empty and sterile as if it had never been used at all.

But even though Stratham carried his laptop with him on the yacht, he didn't seem like the type to carry it that way, in general. He had to have a laptop bag of some kind. A briefcase or a backpack or at least a sling bag. No one carried a bare laptop around all the time. And since Stratham wasn't carrying his bag around the ship, he must have left it somewhere.

Paul went around the room again. There were no drawers in the desk. Remembering all the secret doors he'd already found, he tugged and pushed at the panels on the walls. He found the door to the art gallery, as cleverly hidden as the others on Paloma's deck.

Along the wall behind the desk, he pushed against a panel. It clicked open, revealing several shelves stacked from floor to ceiling. They were all empty. He moved along the wall, clicking panel after panel. All opened to empty shelves. Except one, which held a black leather shoulder bag, the strap lain neatly underneath.

Jackpot.

Paul pulled the bag out and set it on the desk. A large flap buckled over a zip-up pocket, with several compartments inside. The leather was smooth and soft under his fingers. Probably calfskin. As he stroked the bag, Paul could imagine the poor baby cow that was the original owner of the skin. He shuddered. Why someone would kill an animal just to make a fancy bag from its skin was beyond him. Especially these days, when they could do so much with synthetic fibers. Paul was no vegan, not even a vegetarian. But he knew hubris when he saw it. He knew waste.

Looking for anything that might be of use, he rummaged through the compartments. Something that might hold data. An external hard drive or a thumb drive, maybe. A sticky note with a password on it would be nice, but he knew Stratham was not so foolish.

All Paul found were a bunch of connection cables, a power cord and box, a lanyard attached to an ID with a picture of a stern-faced Stratham, and a manila folder containing a sheaf of papers. The ID photo had been taken back when Stratham still had hair.

Paul shoved the ID in his jacket pocket and opened the folder. He riffled through the papers. Each had a picture and a short bio. There weren't enough papers to represent every guest on board, but Paul figured the most important—meaning wealthy—ones were in there. A cheat sheet for Stratham to use in targeting and schmoozing donors. Paul couldn't imagine Stratham schmoozing anyone. But, then again, you didn't get to be campaign finance chairperson for a major presidential contender without having some people skills.

Or some intelligence with protecting data. Paul sighed. He wasn't going to find anything useful in here. Stratham didn't care about leaving his bag in an unlocked office because his bag didn't hold anything of value. Everything of value he kept with him at all times.

He flipped through the papers in the folder, scanning the bio sheets for anything interesting. Tech moguls, media titans, Hollywood bigwigs. It was California, after all. There were a few oil executives, too, and some less specific designations, like *entrepreneur* or *investor*. Those could mean anything, which was exactly why Paul was using *investor* as his own cover story. He was sure there were at least a couple of unsavory characters on board, not the least of which would have been Minsk himself, before he died.

Before he was murdered. Could one of the guests have murdered him?

It was possible. But the crew was cleaning up the messes, and neither the captain nor Paloma seemed particularly perturbed by Minsk's demise. There could be a guest involved, but Paloma and the captain were definitely in on it.

Paul shook his head as he shoved the folder back into the bag. He had to focus on his task. Get Stratham's laptop and get off the ship. As he lifted the bag to put it back on the shelf, he spotted one more pocket on the outside. Paul shoved his hand in and pulled the contents out.

Melantha's diamond choker.

Why the hell would Melantha's choker be in Stratham's bag? And why wouldn't Melantha be more concerned about it?

He thought back to Paloma's salon, to Melantha's ice-cold demeanor, to the casual way Stratham called her "Mel", spoke to her like there was history between them.

Could Stratham be Melantha's ex? That anal-retentive old man? Why would a beauty like Melantha be with a dull pencil pusher like Stratham?

Paul shook his head. Stranger things had happened. He need look no further than Minsk and Paloma themselves. Wealth and power somehow made the most vile of men seem attractive to some women. Paul wouldn't have counted Melantha among those women. But, he didn't really know her at all, did he?

And apparently she and Stratham had broken up, she'd returned her necklace to him, and the feelings between them were still raw.

Paul thought about stealing the necklace. It had to be worth a fortune, several hundred thousand dollars, at least. He knew exactly how to move it. Break it up and sell the stones. He had a number of contacts who would be happy to buy them. And the necklace was right there, ripe for the taking. His fingers practically itched for it.

But no. He'd sworn to himself to break no laws beyond what was absolutely necessary until he'd secured his mother's release. If Paul wound up in jail for some stupid thing, his mother would never be free again. He left the necklace where it was, set the bag back on the shelf, and tucked the leather strap neatly beneath it, just as he'd found it.

Paul closed the cabinet panel with a sigh. Since he was coming up empty in the office, he was going to have to take bigger risks. He was going to have to expose himself.

29

PAUL WOULD HAVE PREFERRED to stay in the shadows, to let the others think he was still tied to a drainpipe in a storage room on the lowest deck. But he had to get to Stratham, and the easiest way to do that was to walk up to him.

But he would need some way to keep the captain and Whitley from immediately locking him up again. He needed a distraction.

He could wait until they docked, until the guests were all leaving, then pinch the laptop from Stratham when Paloma and the captain were saying their obligatory goodbyes. But that left Paul too close to the cops. If the captain radioed ahead, the cops could be waiting on the dock. The captain could bring them on board before the first guests disembarked. And then Paul would be fucked.

He couldn't take that risk. He had to get the laptop and get off the ship before any police got involved.

Paul left the office, checking first to be sure no one was by the stairwell, and rejoined the party in the salon on Deck Four. No better place to hide than in plain sight.

A few of the guests had clearly had too much. One man with a bald head and a comb-over was twirling in circles in the center of the dance floor, a wide cushion around him as the other guests gave him plenty of space. He had taken off his tuxedo coat and undone his bow tie. His shirt was soaked with sweat as he twirled and laughed and shouted for his wife to join him. She looked mortified and did her best to ignore her husband. It was the high-class equivalent of a late night bar brawl, when the men drowning their sorrows had turned belligerent and started to make decisions they would regret in the morning. Those men usually woke up in prison. The bald-headed twirler would wake up the butt of his friends' jokes, ostracized from whatever social circles he ran in. For him, it would amount to the same thing.

While the twirler had clearly had too much, some of the others seemed to have had enough. They slumped in low chairs or at tables, their eyes heavy, staring at the other party-goers. These tended to be the older guests, white-haired and wrinkled, backs hunched and hands skeletal. For them, the party had gone on too long, and they had no way to leave early. Minsk should have arranged for a ferry to bring guests back to the mainland if they wanted to go. Because he didn't, these poor souls were trapped in fundraising purgatory, waiting for release.

But the majority of the guests were still pressing on with their schmoozing, their wheeling and dealing. How many ventures were started that night? How many fortunes won or lost by the conversations had on the yacht that evening? Paul had no idea if that's how big money actually worked, but wasn't that why the rich came to these events? To see and be seen? To rub elbows with other rich folks and hatch schemes to make themselves even richer?

He scanned the crowd for any faces he knew. Paloma, the captain, Whitley.

Melantha.

Paul gulped as he surveyed the crowd. He wasn't sure if he wanted to see Melantha or not. How could he run through so many emotions in just a few hours? He'd gone from indifferent to interested to infatuated to inconsolable to insecure all in one evening. Ridiculous.

Focus. He had to focus.

He scanned the crowd again, looking for the one he really wanted to see: Stratham.

No luck. Stratham was tall enough to have stuck out like a fox in a hen house, but he just wasn't there.

Careful to give the twirler plenty of room, Paul moved through the crowd, onto the deck, then to the rail to look down on the deck below, scanning the crowd as he walked. No sign of Stratham or the others.

He turned and looked up at the deck above him, Paloma's deck. If Stratham wasn't down at the party, he could be up there with Paloma, working through the spreadsheet again. There was no one standing at the rail. Paul would have to go up there himself to be sure.

Paul climbed the spiral stairs once more. He hesitated outside Paloma's salon, his hand hovering over the button to open the doors. He was supposed to be locked up, and by exposing himself now, he would be putting himself at risk. Yes, he needed to find Stratham, but if he just waltzed in to where the others were, they would only lock him up again, tighter and more securely than before.

He pulled his hand back. He needed to find Stratham, but this was not the way to do it. There had to be a better way.

His hand moved of its own accord to pat his left breast.

There was no bulge from what was inside the inner pocket of his tuxedo jacket. The device there folded completely flat. But Paul could feel it, hard 3-D printed resin just waiting to be utilized.

There was a better way, and Paul had just thought of it.

30

THE GLASSES in his pocket were augmented reality glasses he'd stolen from the home of Dr. Christopher Nestrom eight months earlier, in the days after Christmas when Nestrom's family murdered him. Nestrom, tech genius extraordinaire, had nearly perfected his latest creation, one which was bound to revolutionize the world the way his smartphones had in the preceding decades. Nestrom's family, as far as Paul could tell from industry news reports, had never been caught for the murder and was still working to get the prototype to market.

Paul felt a pang in his heart when he thought about those few strange days he'd spent with the family, not because of the theft or even the murder, but because he'd fallen in love—in lust, he supposed, or infatuation—with Nestrom's daughter, Kat. Just like Melantha, Paul—using the name Sam Davis, then— had fallen too hard and too fast for Kat. Ridiculously fast. Though, in his defense, he'd been with Kat for several days, not just a few hours like Melantha.

And he'd gotten over her. It had taken a while, but he'd gotten over her. The fact that she was a murderer helped. The fact that she'd murdered her own father in cold blood helped even more. But it had taken months before Paul could look at another woman again. And he still felt a stab in his heart even now, more than eight months later.

He'd learned a lot in those few days with Kat. And he'd gained even more than knowledge from the experience. He'd gained a prototype version of Nestrom's AR glasses, with the ability to pull in data from sensitive cameras and sensors as well as from any local networks and the internet, synthesize it all, and present it to the wearer in a seamless, intuitive way that pumped an unbelievable richness of detail and information straight into the wearer's brain. Like having the full knowledge of the internet at your command, having eyes all over, being able to see in the dark. The power of the glasses was incredible.

And in all the craziness of the night, Paul had forgotten he was carrying them. But now he was going to use them to his advantage.

He'd spent the months since he stole the glasses figuring out how they worked. The design was very intuitive, one of Nestrom's hallmarks, but the capabilities of the device were many, and it had taken Paul a long time to explore them. With as much as he could do with the glasses now, he still felt like he'd only just begun to scratch the surface.

Because of that, and because of the scandal that would result if he were caught wearing them, he was hesitant to use them too often. The temptation was strong—a device like the glasses made everything easier, even just a trip to the corner market— but Paul resisted. Technology was as much a drug as heroin, and could be nearly as damaging, if taken to the extreme. If any tech- nology would push people to the extreme, these glasses would do it. And Paul refused to become a tech addict.

But this was the time to use the tool he'd brought. Thankful he'd taken the time to raise the curtain before he'd left earlier, he checked through the window of the office across from Paloma's salon, making sure it was still empty, then slipped inside, put on the glasses, and booted them up. The room went completely black. Then the Nestech logo, a blue letter N, floated in front of his eyes for a moment before the outline of the room appeared as white lines on a blue background, like a blueprint, then resolved into full color, with hyper-sharp detail. High-definition graphics and high dynamic range light sensitivity. With these glasses, Paul could look out the window at the mainland glowing miles away in the dark and see not just a thin line of light, but individual buildings, even people walking in front of them. And if he had an internet connection, he could even see their faces, his view enhanced by the feeds from any surveillance cameras on the sides of the buildings.

Fortunately, the yacht had satellite internet. In mere seconds, the glasses found a way to join the local network—more tech magic, courtesy of Dr. Nestrom. Ghostly figures appeared in his view, arrayed in three-dimensional space and realistic perspective around Paul. He could see all of the crew members, caterers, and party guests, a mass of people milling about the yacht, their bodies merging and separating as people on the various decks walked above and below each other.

Paul called up images from the internet for Paloma, Stratham, the captain, and Whitley. He tagged them as people of interest, telling the glasses he wanted special attention paid to those people. Immediately, several of the ghostly figures glowed in yellow, their appearances more solid than the others. The captain was to Paul's left, toward the bow of the ship, standing in place. Probably in the wheelhouse. Whitley's image was smaller and fainter, indicating that she was further away. She looked to be several decks below him, moving in a straight line, possibly headed to the engine room. Paloma and Stratham were behind him to his right, seated in Paloma's salon. The glasses showed them all in real-time in their actual positions around Paul, but with Paul being perfectly and naturally aware of them. No confusion or disorientation at all.

Paul thought of that magical process like this: when you

walk into your kitchen, you know the oven is behind you even though you're not looking at it. You know this because you have an image of the kitchen in your mind. Your mind maintains a map of the space and your position in it. The glasses somehow recreated this sensation, but with information you hadn't learned through experience. They picked up that information from the various camera feeds and internet data, assimilated it, and somehow tricked your brain into positioning it in three-dimensional space in such a way that it felt like you were in your own kitchen, sensing the position of your oven. The technology truly was amazing. It was too bad Nestrom didn't live to perfect it, to see it used by the public.

Paul took a deep breath, then called up an image of Melantha online and marked her as a person of interest. She appeared in his view in the glasses, her image small and faint like Whitley's, moving down a passageway well below him.

Paul had a choice. He could try a simple smash-and-grab. He could bust into Paloma's salon, grab Stratham's laptop before either of them could react, then... Then what? He was on a ship in the middle of the bay. They'd already turned back toward shore, the distant shore lights moving from the port rail to the bow, growing larger by the minute. Paul figured they would be back in twenty minutes, at most. Not enough time to make the grab and escape from a yacht that the others knew far better than he did. Even with the glasses to help him, Paul doubted he could find a way off the ship without being detected before they arrived at the dock and the police got involved.

Paul had to be more subtle.

Or more clever. He saw Whitley's figure move in the glasses, thought back to the engine room. He'd located the generator switches for exactly this reason. A ship gone dark in the middle of the sea with a bunch of rich guests on board would be chaos. And chaos was a thief's best partner, especially if that thief wore Nestrom's AR glasses to help him navigate in the dark.

But that only worked if the crew fell prey to the chaos themselves. If they kept their heads and went straight to the generator switches to turn them on again, Paul would be screwed. And Paul would have to flip the switches, go all the way to Deck Five and into Paloma's salon to steal the laptop, then back down... Where? To a hiding place somewhere?

No, that plan would leave him in the same predicament as a smash-and-grab. He'd be left running around the yacht, trying to stay one step ahead of the crew and the others, hoping for an escape before the ship reached shore. And if the captain were smart—and Paul could tell from the assessing look in his eyes that he was—he would just stop the ship in the water, get the generator back on, then refuse to start up again until Paul was found. He could easily use repairs or diligence as an excuse to the guests for their stoppage, all the while radioing the cops to come and take Paul away, once he was found.

Paul had to secure a way off the ship before he stole the laptop. That meant he had to wait until they got to shore to steal it.

But—again, if the captain were smart—the cops would be waiting at shore for Paul. He couldn't be on the yacht when it docked and the other guests disembarked. He could probably manage to slip away with the crowd, if the captain thought he was still locked up below decks, but he probably couldn't slip away otherwise.

Unless he got the heat off of himself. If he eliminated the captain's ability to use Paul as a scapegoat for Minsk's murder, he could wait until they docked, pinch the laptop, and be gone before anyone even noticed.

The only way to do that would be to solve the damn murder himself.

31

Paul sat down behind the desk in the office on Deck Five, watching carefully in his glasses for any ghostly image that might approach. With the Nestech glasses on, Paul could not be caught unawares. That wouldn't make escaping the ship any easier—didn't matter if you saw them coming when you had nowhere to run—but it made sneaking around very straightforward.

He thought through what he knew. Minsk had been on the owner's deck in the lounge with Paloma when Paul and the captain had been on the deck outside the wheelhouse. A short while later, the server was upstairs bloodying Minsk and being killed while Stratham was downstairs in the office. Then Paloma had been back in the salon with Paul while Stratham went up with Minsk. Finally, Stratham came back down and joined Paul and Paloma before Paul went up and watched Minsk off himself.

Melantha could have gone upstairs to Minsk's deck while Stratham was with Paul and Paloma. The captain or Whitley could have been up there at any time.

Paul hadn't seen anyone else go up to or down from Minsk's deck all night, and Minsk had to have been killed during that window of time. Paul had seen him alive, silhouetted in the window, then seen him fall over the rail ninety minutes later. That was the kill zone. One of those people had killed Minsk during that ninety-minute period, and Paul had to figure out who.

Worse, he had to prove it, and prove it well enough that the captain—or the killer—would be more worried about what Paul might tell the police than they would be about framing him as the killer.

Paloma had motive, naturally. Her husband was a monster. And she'd recently learned just how bad of a monster he really was. Would that drive her to murder? Maybe, especially if she thought her wealth would allow her to get away with it. Hell, she might have even hired the assassin to do Minsk in for her.

Where had she been while Minsk was tousling with the assassin? Had she already been downstairs on Deck Five? Had she been on Deck Six, helping the assassin somehow? Perhaps she'd stayed upstairs with Minsk, making sure he was on the top deck alone until the appointed time. Most likely, she then would have gone down to her own rooms to create an alibi while her assassin did the dirty work.

Only Minsk was too strong, even at his age. Too strong, too experienced, and too ruthless. The assassin dealt Minsk a blow —maybe even a killing blow—to the chest, and a nasty blow to the head, but she'd paid for it with her life.

And then what? Stratham had gone upstairs. That had to have been after the struggle with the assassin. Paul had seen her go up at least ten minutes earlier. That meant that Stratham must have seen Minsk, bloody and wounded. And then... he'd come downstairs to see Paloma? No alarm in his eyes. No calls for help. Nothing.

Paul thought back to the moment when Stratham had entered Paloma's salon. What had been their exchange? Something like *All good, Vern?* from Paloma. To which Stratham had replied *Yes, Mrs. Minsk. All good.* Had Paloma known Minsk would be attacked? Had she sent Stratham to confirm the deed? If so, why had Stratham said all was good when Minsk wasn't dead yet? Had he delivered the poison to finish Minsk off? Why would Stratham want Minsk dead?

And then there was the captain and the first officer. They'd cleaned up the body and gone about their business with barely the blink of an eye. Were they in the habit of cleaning corpses off the deck? With Minsk as their master, it was possible. But surely they would be surprised to see Minsk himself on the slab. Unless they knew about it beforehand.

The thought crossed Paul's mind that they could all be involved, working together. It wouldn't be the first time. Paul's lips tingled as his mind flashed back to the previous Christmas. One last kiss in a back doorway. A long, lonely walk across a snow-covered field. He pressed his lips together to chase the tingle away.

What really killed Minsk? Was it the gunshot or the poison? Or had it been the fall? Paul would have to see the body to be sure. But he had no idea where the crew had stored it.

Paul realized with a start that he knew just how to find out.

32

GETTING DOWN to the submersible room had been so easy, Paul wished he'd thought to wear the Nestech glasses earlier. He could have finished the whole job before they'd left the harbor.

But he wouldn't have found the data he needed. Even without Minsk's murder, his original plan had been shot to hell when Minsk's computer terminal turned up nothing useful. Glasses or no glasses, Paul would still have been scrambling for a new approach.

And even with the glasses, he wouldn't have known who to avoid. He certainly knew who to avoid now.

It had been a bit of a long shot, but Paul had pulled up a picture of Minsk from the internet and labeled him a person of interest within the operating system of the Nestech glasses. He didn't know if the glasses would be able to locate a corpse.

But they did. With less than a second of delay, a new figure appeared in Paul's display, prostrate and glowing deep red four decks below where Paul had been standing in the office outside Paloma's salon on Deck Five. Apparently, the Nestech glasses highlighted living people in yellow and dead people in red. Seemed an odd distinction to build into a system, but then Christopher Nestrom had been an odd man.

Regardless, it worked to Paul's advantage now. He'd floated down the central stairs like a ghost, timing his movements to the movements of others he observed in the glasses, pausing only once near the bottom of the stairs to allow Whitley to pass from the forward passageway to the engine room before Paul slipped behind her to the submersible room.

Paul noticed that Melantha had gone back up to the party. He still couldn't figure out her place in all of this. A part of him hoped she had no place, that she was innocent of any wrongdoing. But he knew that was personal bias clouding his judgment. All night long, Melantha had been clutching a tumbler that Paul had only seen in Minsk's office on Deck Six. She had to have gotten it there, and she had to have gotten it before Minsk had been killed. She was involved. Paul just hadn't figured out how. Yet.

The smell of seawater permeated the submersible room with a smell that was almost tactile. Though the room was cool, Paul could feel the seawater on his skin, could taste the salt on his tongue the moment he stepped through the door onto the platform that traversed the space.

He crossed a short causeway to the deck of the submersible. The deck bobbed and rolled gently in the pool of seawater sequestered beneath the ship. The rough texture of the deck allowed Paul to keep his balance. It was genius, really, to leave a slice of the hull open to the ocean beneath, creating a simple way for the submersible to enter and exit the ship.

Paul had a moment of odd disorientation as he adjusted to the movement of the sub. It had a different rhythm than the rest of the ship. For a brief moment when he stepped on the top deck, Paul felt like the world around him was drifting away, moving at a speed he could not control or catch.

But the moment passed and he regained his bearings. And his focus. According to the glasses, Minsk's body was just below Paul, inside the submersible.

Paul stepped down the ladder and through the airlock into the main chamber of the sub. As he had first seen through the long window overhead, the interior of the sub looked and felt like an old English study, with leather armchairs and mahogany detailing on a wide railing that spanned the length of both walls. A full bar was set into the wall on the far side, of course. Paul half expected a butler in white vest and black tails to emerge from the far hatch and offer his apologies that Master Minsk had been unexpectedly detained, but would sir care for a spot of sherry while he waited?

Paul walked slowly through the room. The walls curved out from the ceiling before curving back at the floor, leaving the impression that Paul was walking through the barrel of an old glass syringe. The water all around was dark and impenetrable, lit only by thin strands of light filtering down from the spotlights in the submersible room. When Paul looked out, he saw himself reflected in the glass.

He moved slowly through the leather chairs, grouped in pairs before the window, small tables between them for whiskey glasses and ashtrays. Paul could only imagine what it would have been like trapped in a sub with a dozen rich men drinking Scotch and smoking cigars. It must have been like the back rooms in saloons in the Old West, where the real money games were played. The air choked with smoke and inflated egos, where a winning hand was as likely to be paid out in bullets as in dollars.

He stepped through the hatch at the far end of the submersible into a short cylindrical collar. Narrow doors stood on either side. A ladder beside the door to his right led to the deck above. Ahead, he saw the controls for the sub, set into a bulbous end cap that offered the pilot a full 180-degree view above, below, and to the sides. The control panels glowed in the dark space, green and red buttons and a blank radar screen providing the only illumination. Paul's face reflected in the glass had a greenish horror-movie cast to it.

Paul had walked from one end of the sub to the other. The one thing he hadn't seen was the one thing he'd come to see. Minsk's body was nowhere to be found.

Yet the glasses Paul wore told him that Minsk was right beside him. And the body wasn't prostrate anymore, but was standing upright.

Paul looked around, looked more closely at the hatch he'd stepped through. Two doors were set into the walls of the hatch, one on either side. According to the glasses, Minsk was behind one of them.

Paul took a deep breath and pulled open the left-hand door, opening it slowly, carefully, one hand up to catch Minsk's body if it fell.

It didn't fall. It just stared back at Paul. Whoever had moved the body had righted the neck so that the head faced forward, but they hadn't bothered to close the eyes. Minsk's eyes were the same dead eyes Paul had seen from the rail six decks above. Where before they had seemed accusing, now they seemed sad. Disappointed, even. Maybe they hadn't wanted to die after all. Maybe they'd expected Paul to have found the true killer by now.

Or maybe Paul had been on the damn yacht too long and had finally started to lose his mind.

He pulled his cellphone from his pocket and flipped on the flashlight. As he'd thought, the wound on Minsk's head was bloody, but superficial. Nasty, but not a fatal gash.

Paul pushed aside Minsk's suit jacket with the back of one hand and bent close to examine the blood there. The shirt was crusted now, the blood largely dry, making the shirt stand stiff, casting harsh, straight-edged shadows against Minsk's bulging gut. Despite the stiffness, Paul could clearly see that the shirt itself was untouched. There were no holes or tears in the fabric beneath the blood.

Paul's mind spun with confusion. The blood wasn't Minsk's. There was no bullet wound or stab to the heart. All of the blood that soaked Minsk's shirt must have come from the assassin when Minsk stabbed her, or when he dragged her body to the side of the helipad. Whatever happened in that attack, the assassin hadn't killed Minsk.

Which meant someone else had.

Paul closed the door, sealing Minsk back inside. Out of curiosity, he opened the opposite door. The assassin's body was there, standing at rest the same way Minsk's body had been. This time, someone had taken the time to close the woman's eyes. Where Minsk had seemed sad about his fate, the assassin just looked like she was sleeping.

But she wasn't sleeping. She was dead. And someone had gone to a lot of trouble to cover up two murders.

"See anything interesting?"

Whitley's voice startled Paul. He'd been so focused on examining the bodies he'd completely tuned out the movements of the people around him in the glasses. How he could have done so, he didn't know, for Whitley's yellow image glowed life-size in his peripheral vision. She was standing in the hatch, blocking him in.

Glasses or no glasses, Paul was trapped on a tiny sub with a potential murderer, and he had no way to escape.

33

"ACTUALLY, YES," said Paul, keeping his voice calm. He was shooting for a breezy tone, but wound up sounding merely conversational. Close enough.

He closed the door on the assassin's corpse and turned to face First Officer Whitley. Though the light in the cabin was dim, he could see her well enough. Paul realized this was the first time he'd really gotten a good look at the woman.

She was tall and muscular, with a no-nonsense air about her that suggested to Paul she knew at least three ways in their current environment to kill him swiftly and dispose of his body. High competence and low compunction. That was Whitley's vibe.

She held no weapon. Her stance was non-threatening. She was just standing in the hatch like she would stand in line at the lunch counter. Yet Paul felt like she was holding a gun aimed at his gut.

Paul studied her angular features. They seemed vaguely familiar.

"Do enlighten me, Mr. Baker," she said with a slight smile.

In the small space, surrounded by the insular hush that comes from being underwater, Paul detected the faintest hint of an accent in her voice. A heaviness in her vowels. A glottal scrape in her consonants. Paul guessed Eastern European. Maybe Russian.

It came to him in a flash of recognition. When it did, he couldn't believe he hadn't seen it before.

"You're the captain's daughter," he said.

The smile dropped from Whitley's face. In the pale green light from the console behind Paul, her face seemed to blanch.

"Granddaughter," she said, her accent thickening. Her mouth twisted. "I'm younger than I look."

Whitley and her grandfather, working together on the yacht. It might have been a heartwarming story in other circumstances. The older generation passing down a love of the sea and a life-time of nautical knowledge. An aging captain getting to know his young granddaughter in the waning years of his life.

In this case, it seemed more like a bitter old man infecting his kin with a burning hatred of the wealthy despot who oppressed him. And maybe plotting murder with his grand-daughter. The captain had made no bones about his dislike of Minsk. He'd suggested some history between them, some debt that was owed or some power imbalance. Paul had the sense it went beyond mere employer-employee disgruntlement.

"What did you find, Mr. Baker?" Whitley asked, stepping through the hatchway into the collar.

She was mere feet from Paul now, and her body blocked the ladder to the deck above. Not that Paul would have tried to escape. Whitley could have easily stopped him, unless he somehow incapacitated her first. From the look of her stolid frame and her now-scowling countenance, he doubted he could do that.

"I found the bodies you stashed," he said, again shooting for breezy, again falling short and landing on a conversational tone instead. He pointed to the door on his right. "Minsk and"—he pointed left—"Minsk's assassin."

"Assassin?" scoffed Whitley. "Don't you mean server?" She smirked at him. "A poor, unfortunate member of the catering staff in the wrong place at the wrong time, caught up in a murder that had nothing to do with her?"

Paul raised one eyebrow and Whitley's smirk straightened.

"The funny thing is that, aside from his head, Minsk doesn't have any wounds on his body," Paul said. "None that I could see, anyway."

He looked at Whitley. Her expression had gone blank.

"No gunshot wound," he continued. "No knife wound. No fatal wounds at all."

Still, Whitley's expression didn't change.

"Which means that the assassin didn't kill Minsk."

"You killed Minsk."

Paul sighed. "We both know that's not true. But someone on this ship did." He tilted his head. "Maybe even you."

Whitley didn't flinch at the accusation.

If the assassin hadn't killed Minsk, if he hadn't died from wounds from their fight, then he had to have died from the poison he ingested. The blood loss from his head wound may have disoriented him, but he wouldn't have bled out from it. Someone had poisoned Minsk, and the poison had killed him.

An idea came to Paul. He smiled at Whitley.

"I don't know who killed Minsk," he said, "but I think I know how to find out."

34

PAUL STOOD at the rail of the small weather deck outside the lounge on Deck Six, waiting for the others to arrive. He no longer needed his Nestech glasses to see the lights of the shore. They were large and bright, their yellow glow surrounding him as the yacht drew as close to shore as it safely could, given its size and the depth of the harbor. On the deck below him, crew members were scurrying about, preparing to dock with the support ship that would ferry the partygoers to land. Though he couldn't see them, Paul knew the guests would be gathering as well, moving en masse toward the stern of the ship where the ferry would dock, fatigue creeping into their countenances, the glitter and glamour of the evening already beginning to fade.

Paul listened to the burble of the hot tub behind him. He turned and leaned against the rail. Steam wafted up from the roiling water into the cool night air. Again, the blue-green color of the water caught his eye through the glass wall between the treads of the stairs. Such simple beauty amid such extravagant waste.

In his memories, like an unwelcome guest, he saw Minsk calmly stepping up those hot tub stairs, stepping stiff-legged like a zombie through the steaming water, then tipping himself over the rail.

Paul shivered and moved inside. The door slid shut behind him with a soft hiss.

Whitley stood to one side of the room—the side nearest the stairway, Paul noticed, ready to stop him if he tried to run for it. The captain stood on the opposite side. There were only two chairs in the room. Paloma sat in one, beside the captain, Melantha in the chair opposite.

One more person to arrive.

At last, Stratham came around the corner and stood beside Melantha's chair, his ever-present laptop in his hand, clutched at his waist.

"What's this?" he said. "The ferry is almost here, and I have some last-minute business to attend with the guests before they disembark."

"This will only take a moment," Paul said. "And thank you all for coming."

"It's always a pleasure to hear your stories, Mr. Baker," said Paloma, her voice practically a purr. "I'll be sorry to see the police take you away."

A thousand retorts flooded Paul's mind, but he kept his mouth shut and nodded at Paloma.

"I know the prevailing wisdom is that I killed Devin Minsk this evening. Pushed him over the rail"—he pointed behind him with a thumb over his shoulder—"and watched him fall to his death."

"And we have many witnesses who will attest that to the police," said the captain, "including myself."

"The police will be on the ferry, no?" Paloma asked the captain.

The captain looked to Whitley.

"The police have been informed," she said. "They will be waiting at the dock."

The fact that the police weren't coming to the yacht made Paul wonder what, exactly, they'd been informed of. If it were murder, or even just a death onboard, they would undoubtedly have sent a police boat to the yacht. If they were willing to wait for the ferry to dock at the pier, they must have been fed a different story.

"If you're suggesting that they're waiting for me," Paul said, "then I will be happy to cooperate and tell them everything I know."

He waited, looking at each of the faces before him in turn. They all looked back quietly, holding his gaze. Whitley's face was like stone, impassive. Stratham looked annoyed. Melantha merely curious. Paloma seemed to be enjoying every moment of Paul's show. And the captain, well, he wore the same haughty look of barely restrained irritation Paul had seen on his face every single moment since he'd first met the man. Resting bitch face had nothing on Captain William Constance.

"And what is it you think you know?" said Paloma, breaking the long silence at last.

"I'll tell you in just a moment," Paul said, "but first, I feel it only right that we should honor the dead."

He turned to the small table to his left. Before gathering the others, with Whitley watching him closely, he'd collected the bottle of vodka and a tray of glasses from the bar in the office, a tray of octagonal-shaped tumblers like the one Melantha had carried with her all night long, each filled with two ice cubes. Paul glanced at her and noticed that she hadn't brought it up with her this time. The tray now sat on the table.

He picked up the bottle of vodka, the same bottle someone had laced with poison earlier in the night, held it toward the others so each could clearly see.

"I found this just now in the office down the hall. As I understand it, Mrs. Minsk, your husband was partial to vodka, was he not?"

Paloma scoffed. "Partial to it? He practically bathed in it."

Paul nodded. "Then it seems only fitting that we toast his memory with a glass of vodka, don't you agree?"

A venomous scowl covered the captain's face.

"Toast his memory?" Paloma said. "No, I won't toast his memory. But I'll gladly toast his absence."

The scowl lifted. The captain nodded once in agreement.

"Very well," said Paul. He pulled the stopper from the vodka bottle and poured some into each glass, then carried the tray around the room, stopping to let each person to choose a glass for themselves. When they all had theirs in hand, Paul raised the glass that remained.

"Would anyone care to do the honors?"

"This is your funeral, Mr. Baker," said the captain. "Let's get on with it."

"To Mr. Devin Minsk," said Paul, lifting his glass. With a nod toward Paloma, he said, "May our lives be happy in his absence."

He had no idea what to say in that moment, and he didn't care. He didn't give a shit about Minsk. He just wanted an excuse to get everyone to drink. And he hoped a shot of vodka and a toast to a dead man, even one as vile as Minsk, would do the trick.

The others murmured unintelligible things and tossed back their drinks.

"Blech," said Paloma, wrinkling her face in disgust and looking at her empty tumbler with suspicion. "What the hell is this?"

"This is not vodka," muttered the captain as he peered into his own glass.

Whitley, too, considered the empty glass in her hand with confusion.

But Paul wasn't focused on any of them. He'd expected each of them to react the way they did.

Paul was focused on Vernon Stratham.

And he was shocked by what he saw.

Stratham held his glass before him, tilting his head, an expression of bafflement on his face.

"It's water," he said. "Lukewarm tap water."

Paul had expected Stratham to balk at drinking the vodka, vodka Paul was sure he'd laced with poison. He'd half-expected Stratham to shout out, to stop the others from drinking what would be a lethal dose.

Instead, Stratham had tossed the drink back without a second thought. Just like all the others.

All the others except one.

Melantha.

35

PAUL SHIFTED his gaze from Stratham and settled it on Melantha. She gazed back at him from her seat, the tumbler in her lap, still full of water from the tap in Minsk's office.

While Whitley watched the passageway to make sure he didn't escape, Paul had gone to the office to collect the vodka and the tumblers. He'd dumped out the poisoned vodka, rinsed the bottle thoroughly, and filled it with cool water from the sink.

He wasn't a murderer, after all. He didn't want to kill anyone. But he figured he'd flush out the one who did. Whoever didn't drink, whoever stopped the others from drinking, would be the one who'd poisoned the vodka and killed Minsk.

The last person he expected that to be was Melantha.

And that surprise must have registered on Paul's face. Melantha, staring back at him, raised her eyebrows as a smile twisted her lips.

"Do you have something to say to me, Paul?" she asked.

Paul shook his head and worked his mouth for a moment, trying to form words to match the thoughts in his head. But there were too many thoughts, too many feelings, all piling on top of one another. Far too much to express.

"I think what Paul is failing to say is that he thinks I killed

Minsk," said Melantha in a calm, pleasant tone of voice. "He thinks I poisoned his vodka."

"Did you?" asked Paloma.

Melantha looked at her and smiled. "Of course."

Paloma stared at Melantha for a long moment, then reached across the space between their chairs, put a hand on Melantha's wrist, and shook it once. "Good for you." She shook Melantha's wrist once more, firmly, and looked around the room. "Good for all of us, I expect."

"You poisoned the vodka?" said the captain, looking at his empty glass with suspicion. He looked at Paul. "And you served it to us?"

"I dumped out the poisoned vodka first," he said.

"And therefore the evidence." Melantha batted her eyelashes at him.

"I'm not here to get anyone arrested," said Paul. "Unlike the rest of you." He glared at the captain, who stared impassively back. "But I will tell the police everything I know if you let them arrest me."

"What, exactly, do you know, Mr. Baker?" asked Paloma. "You promised you'd tell us, and I, for one, cannot wait to hear it."

"I know the captain owes Minsk money. Gambling debts. He's working here as an indentured servant." The captain's eyes went flat and his lips pursed. "No love lost there. Plenty of motive for murder."

"But no proof," said Whitley.

"And Whitley is his granddaughter. Her motive is to free the captain."

"A family drama," said Paloma with glee. "Like a soap opera. So American. Or, in this case, Russian."

"I know Paloma hated her husband," Paul continued, "stood to inherit his fortune if he died."

"Motive isn't murder," said Stratham with a tone of bored assurance. "You don't know anything."

"I know Vernon Stratham hired an assassin to pose as a server and kill Minsk."

"Vern, did you do that?" asked Paloma.

His assurance suddenly gone, Stratham squirmed where he stood. "She failed. Got herself killed, instead."

"And left a mess for my crew to clean up," grumbled the captain into his empty tumbler.

"I didn't think you had it in you, Vern." Paloma nodded at him, clearly impressed.

"*Another* mess," the captain continued. He glared at Stratham. "You think this ship sails itself?"

Stratham straightened at Paloma's praise, his squirming stopped, and ignored the captain. "Again," he said to Paul, "no proof."

"And I know what actually killed Minsk was the poison in his vodka. Vodka that Melantha served to him."

Everyone spoke at once, the refrain now well established. "But you have no—"

"For this one I do," Paul raised his voice over them. He pulled down his jacket sleeve and used it to hold up the glass he'd carried in his pocket all evening. "Poison residue, fingerprints, all kinds of evidence here, I'm sure. And on the vodka bottle." He gestured at the bottle on the table beside him. "Motives may not be murder, but they will raise all kinds of suspicion." He looked around the room at the others. "Cops are curious people. Do you really want them poking around in your lives?"

No one looked away, but there were no glib retorts, either.

"Then you don't want to hand me over to the police." He slid the evidence-laden tumbler back into his pocket. "Like I said, I'll tell them everything I know."

"From what I understand," said Melantha softly, "poison isn't what killed Minsk." She looked up at Paul, her face open, open and beautiful. "He died from a broken neck."

"Technically, that makes you the killer," said Whitley to Paul.

"I didn't push him over the rail."

"Oh really?" Paloma smiled broadly. "We have several eyewitnesses who say you did. Several members of the crew, not to mention the captain himself. And me. We saw Minsk fall. We looked up, and there you were, leaning over the edge."

Paul stared at her. She smiled sweetly back.

"Mutually assured destruction." Paul laughed. The situation was so ridiculous, he couldn't help himself.

"It's the Russian way," growled the captain.

"And it earns us a detente," said Stratham.

Silence fell over the lot of them.

"So what do we do now?" asked Melantha.

"We go home." The captain's tone suggested more of an order than an answer.

Paloma stood. "Thank you for a very interesting evening, Mr. Baker. These events are normally so dull." She wrapped Paul in a warm embrace. He was too stunned to react. She turned to Stratham. "You throw one hell of a fundraiser, Vern. I'll give you that."

"Your yacht, your fundraiser. I'm just here to collect the checks."

"And how much did you collect this evening?"

Stratham opened his laptop, tapped a few buttons, and checked his screen. "Just under three million," he said. "On top of the fifty million donated before the guests arrived."

Paloma crossed to stand before Stratham, put her arm over his shoulder. "Fifty-three million should buy me an AG who looks the other way once in a while."

Stratham closed his laptop and sighed. "I'm sure Attorney General Jenkins will be most appreciative of your strong support for his campaign."

Paloma patted Stratham on the shoulder like she was patting an obedient Labrador. "I'm sure he will, Vern."

"Are we done?" the captain asked Paul. He gestured toward his first officer. "Some of us still have work to do."

Paul nodded. The captain crossed toward the door. "Wait," Paul said. "What exactly did you tell the police? I don't want them arresting me when I step onto the dock."

The captain looked to Whitley, who cocked one eyebrow at Paul. "I asked them to be at the dock when the guests disembark."

"Did you tell them why?"

Whitley shrugged. "It's late. The guests are rich. I don't need to tell them why."

"In that case," said Paul with a broad smile, "we're done. Thank you all for coming."

The captain grumbled something Paul couldn't make out, but he was pretty sure it wasn't *have a good evening.*

As he turned away, Paul said, "Wait. One more thing."

The captain and Whitley looked back at him.

"What will you do with the bodies? People will want to know what happened to Minsk."

"Mr. Baker, I'm Russian. We know how to dispose of bodies." He leered at Paul. "Why do you think borscht is red?"

Paul reeled back in horror, his stomach suddenly turning cartwheels.

"Beets, Mr. Baker. Beets." The captain laughed, the sound low and full of joy. It rang around the room like church bells on a clear morning. Paul didn't know which was more shocking: the image of bloody borscht a moment ago or the image of the captain laughing so hard right now. The captain pointed one finger at Paul, the other hand clutching his stomach. "Your face," he said, his own face turning almost as red as a bowl of borscht. "Such classic."

He and Whitley went down the stairs, the sounds of the captain's raucous laughter echoing back to Paul. Paloma steered Stratham, still clutching his laptop, down behind them.

Melantha stood, smoothed her dress, and stared at Paul. She spread her hands at her sides.

"Well?" she asked after a moment. "You going to tell me I'm a bad person? Turn me in to the cops?"

"No," said Paul softly.

"Minsk was a horrible human being."

"I know."

"Do you? He killed innocents, abused his wife, bribed government officials, fomented war and genocide just to boost his sales. And he got richer and richer as a result. Killing him was a good thing. I did the world a favor. Not to mention Paloma."

"Is that the real reason you did it? Because you want to get in with her?"

Melantha's eyes flashed with anger. "Did you not hear what I just said?" When Paul just stared back at her, the anger cooled. She shook her head in irritation, admitting to Paul's accusation. "Getting closer to Paloma was just one reason." She pressed her lips so tightly together that Paul could see them whiten even under her lipstick. "Paloma wasn't the only one Minsk abused." Her hands clenched into fists. Rage filled her eyes, then quickly cooled again, hardened to steel. "I don't regret what I did."

Paul held her gaze for a long moment. Had Minsk abused Melantha, too? How much of a monster was that man?

Paul started to reach toward Melantha, to hold her or comfort her somehow. The steel in her gaze stopped him cold. She didn't need comfort from Paul. She was a fighter, and she'd just won her war. One of them, at least.

Paul sighed. "I just don't want to have to deal with the police. I don't care about Minsk."

Melantha furrowed her brow. "Why not?"

Paul shook his head at her, confused by the question.

"You don't care that I killed someone?" said Melantha.

"Tried to kill someone," Paul corrected. "It was the fall that killed him."

Melantha's eyes went wide. She barked a quick laugh and shook her head. "You're crazy, man. I can't seem to figure you out. As soon as I think I've got you pegged, you go and do something that doesn't fit." She stopped and looked him over from head to toe and back again, then sauntered up to him, one long leg at a time slipping out from under her satin gown. She ran her hands down Paul's lapels, then tugged him close. "I guess that's why I like you so much," she whispered, her breath hot against his ear.

The scent of her perfume intoxicated him. Even at the end of a long evening, the floral and citrus made his head swoon. His mouth went dry and his head suddenly felt light, the blood rushing to other parts of his body.

"Why—" Paul began. His words stuck in his dry throat. He swallowed hard and tried again. "Why did you sleep with me earlier?"

Melantha arched back to look at his face, disbelief on her own. She stepped back, still holding Paul's lapels, but now at arm's length. Seeing that his question was serious, she scoffed and shook her head.

"You know, if I were a guy and you were some hot piece of ass, no one would think twice about me fucking you downstairs during a party. Hell, they'd buy me drinks, slap me on the back and ask for details. But because I'm a woman, suddenly there has to be a fucking inquisition just because I felt horny and thought you were fine."

"That's all it was? You were horny and I was there?"

Melantha shook her head at Paul again, genuine puzzlement on her face. "We're both adults," she said. "Both consenting." She held up her hands. "At least, I didn't hear you complaining earlier."

"No, no." Paul shook his head. He took a deep breath and

shut the door on the pain in his heart. "No complaints." Shut the door and locked it. He gave Melantha a prim smile. "No complaints at all."

Melantha's indignant expression softened. She stepped closer to Paul again, put one hand on his chest, searched his eyes with her own. Paul avoided her gaze for a moment, then gave up and let himself fall into her eyes one more time.

"Oh my God," she whispered. She closed her eyes for a long moment, swallowed once, then looked at Paul squarely.

Her deep, dark eyes stopped his heart, but just once. Just once.

"We just met," she said softly. "I've only known you for a couple of hours. That's not enou—" She stammered. "How could you be—" She laughed softly, looked down to collect her thoughts. "I do like you, Paul," she said, smoothing his tuxedo shirt. "Maybe we can get a drink sometime." She laughed out loud then. "No poison, I promise."

"I thought you hated drinking."

"I'm willing to make an exception," she smiled, "this one time."

Paul pulled in a deep breath, then let it out slowly. Really, why was every beautiful woman in his life a fucking murderer? He battled himself. His heart wanted desperately to love some-one, anyone, and to be loved by them. But he couldn't impose a fantasy onto the real world. The real world was anything but fantastic.

"I don't think so, Melantha," he said. "But I do wish you well."

Melantha searched his face for a moment, then nodded slowly. She patted his chest. "Okay," she said. "Okay. But Paul?"

She slid her hand across his chest, ran it down his side, sending warm shivers through his body.

"Hmm?" said Paul, his eyes starting to glaze.

When Melantha's hand reached Paul's waist, instead of

continuing down, she moved it to his jacket pocket. She pulled the tumbler out and held it up between them.

"I'm gonna need this back," she said. She turned and strutted from the room just as she'd strutted from the salon a few hours earlier: slow and sexy, watching over her shoulder as Paul watched her leave.

Paul closed his eyes and groaned as his body ached for her touch again. He pulled in another long slow breath, let it out and did it again, then a third time.

As he let out the third breath, he opened his eyes. His mind was focused once more.

He'd avoided the threat of the police and made his peace with Melantha, but Paul still had work to do. Stratham's laptop was still somewhere on the ship.

And Paul had to get it before he left.

36

PAUL STOOD ALONE in the lounge on Deck Six. He slipped on the Nestech glasses and waited for them to boot up, then called up the location of Vernon Stratham. Stratham was downstairs amidships on Deck Three, approaching the mass of partygoers as they grouped toward the rear of the yacht, where the ferry would soon dock to bring them back to shore.

Would Stratham ride back with the guests, or would he stay on the yacht? Paul couldn't recall seeing Stratham on the ferry when he'd ridden it over at the start of the evening, but that meant nothing. Stratham could have arrived earlier and still planned to return with the other guests to continue one last round of schmoozing and bribe—sorry, *campaign contribution* —collection.

Paul would have to play it loose, play it by ear. Improvise. Theft was like music, Paul's father used to say. You needed to practice your ass off to learn the tunes, the scales, the chords. Then you needed to get on the stage and forget all of it. Just live in the moment, react to what life gave you. And improvise when things didn't go as planned.

Because things never went as planned.

Paul took a deep breath and headed down the stairs. He

curled down to Deck Three. Stratham would be behind the sliding doors across from the landing, standing with Paloma and Melantha amid the throng of guests moving toward the stern of the ship.

But Paul didn't stop on Deck Three. He kept going down two more levels until he reached Deck One.

Where the engine room was.

Before getting off the stairs, he checked the location of the captain and Whitley. As expected, the captain was in the wheel-house. Probably coordinating with the pilot of the ferry. Paul had expected Whitley to be there, too, but her name came up in Paul's screen beside a yellow-glowing image directly behind him and nearly full-size. Startled, he spun around, but saw only a blank wall.

Whitley was in the next room over. The submersible room. Through the wall, Paul heard the electric whir of some kind of cable winch, followed by a blast of water, churning and bubbling.

Of course. The sub. Whitley was taking out the submersible with the bodies on board. Probably dumping it somewhere in the deep ocean where no one but the bottom feeders would ever find them.

The Russians know how to dispose of a body, after all.

In his glasses, Whitley's figure sank below the level of the deck, then moved quickly away, growing smaller in Paul's view as she piloted the submersible away from the yacht, away from shore, toward the night sea.

With everyone's position accounted for, Paul was in the clear.

He turned to the engine room. In his glasses, he saw the two crew members still in there working, their bodies appeared as small, pale shapes behind the wall. Paul pulled a pair of head-phones from the hooks beside the door. He'd may have missed the captain's briefing, but he'd learned his lesson. From now on, he would always wear ear protection in the engine room.

Even if he only intended to slip into the control room for a moment.

He wouldn't have long. No more than a minute, at most. He would have to time it perfectly.

He had one plan, Plan A, and it depended on Stratham staying on the yacht. That was Paul's hope, and it seemed the most likely. Stratham hadn't come in with the guests, so Paul hoped he wouldn't leave with them either.

His plan was a simple tap-and-go. He'd go up the ladder, come at Stratham from the stern to disorient him and get him looking in the wrong direction, nip the laptop, then go back down the central stairs, through to the stern again, and out to the ferry before they knew what hit them. One big loop that would leave Stratham's laptop hidden in Paul's jacket, Stratham looking desperately in the center of the ship for a thief, and Paul slowly chugging away on the ferry toward home. Paul would have to time it perfectly, both the grab and the ferry, but the glasses would give him an advantage.

Plan B would go into play if Stratham took the ferry with the others. He could still steal the laptop, but it would make Paul's getaway much more difficult, and potentially very messy. And it would depend on his driver, Jack, for that plan to come off. Only Jack wasn't aware of the plan, Jack wasn't involved in the plan, Jack wasn't prepared for the plan. He was just a driver, someone Paul had hired to take him to the marina and back. No preparation meant no plan. And while Paul knew that every plan fell apart eventually, he still preferred to have one in place.

So Plan B was no plan at all. Plan A was the only plan.

Not great, but Paul had little choice. The sub was gone. Once the ferry left, Paul would have no way off the yacht, unless he wanted to swim to shore. He didn't.

He stood outside the door to the engine room, the low hum of the engines coming through the wall despite the heavy soundproofing. The central staircase to his back, Paul monitored the movements of everyone on board through his Nestech glasses. He could see the ferry approaching, nearly there. The crew was already extending the floating bridge off the back of the yacht. The guests were crowding closer, eager to get back to shore and go home. It was after one in the morning, already. Way past bedtime for most of these guests.

Stratham was still moving among the throng, probably shaking hands and giving last-minute thanks or pitches for more donations. But it looked like he was moving backward, away from the docking point.

It looked like Paul could be in luck. Plan A might come off after all.

Once the ferry docked, the passengers began to shuffle their way across the bridge. Paul waited until half the group was across, took three deep breaths, and snapped the headphones over his ears. Immediately, the sound of the engines went silent.

He made sure the crew members in the engine room were looking the other way, opened the door to the control room, scanned the wall quickly, and found the four generator switches.

Paul knew he wouldn't have much time. The crew was too good, too experienced. He'd have forty seconds, at most. He would have to move fast.

With one more deep breath, Paul threw all four generator switches at once.

37

BETWEEN THE SOUNDPROOF control room and the headphones he wore, Paul couldn't have heard the engine noise anyway. But in that moment, he knew he wouldn't have heard them if he were standing right beside them.

In that moment, the entire yacht went dead.

Engines, navigation equipment, radios.

And most importantly, lights.

With the generators off, there was a total blackout on board.

And the clock was already ticking.

Paul darted back out of the control room and raced up the twisting central staircase, watching in his glasses for signs of anyone coming in his direction.

Five seconds had passed in the blink of an eye.

So far, no one had moved an inch. Still processing what had happened.

Good. The longer the confusion lasted, the more time Paul had.

He hit the landing on Deck Two and ran. He could see that Stratham was still above and in front of him on Deck Three, standing amid the throng of guests, which jiggled like bees in a hive just waking up from the smoker. Paul could imagine the startled shrieks when the lights had gone out, the shouts of panicked indignation in the darkness, the odd bit of nervous laughter when light didn't immediately return.

Ten seconds.

Paul raced through Deck Two. Navigating the pitch darkness would have taken forever, but the Nestech glasses made it as easy as strolling in the afternoon sun. Through the theater, past the gym, through the lounge—he ignored the twinge in his chest when he saw the couch where he and Melantha had been —to the room with the indoor pool.

Fifteen seconds.

The pool looked eerie black in the glasses. The water shimmered ghostly grey in his viewscreen as it lapped lazily with the waves and the rocking of the ship. Paul was directly below where the guests had congregated before boarding the ferry. Half were still there. Their jiggling had become more orderly. Someone, possibly Stratham but more likely Paloma—the captain was still in the wheelhouse—would be shouting orders in a calm but commanding tone, asking everyone to stay calm while the crew corrected a minor malfunction.

Twenty seconds.

Paul took the stairs two at a time from the pool room to Deck Three. He looked up, scanned quickly through the images for Stratham. He found Paloma above and behind him, outside the salon.

The guests were moving toward the ferry.

Melantha stood beside Paloma. Paul kept scanning for Stratham.

Twenty-five seconds.

He burst through the door at the top of the stairs, burst onto Deck Three.

And nearly knocked an elderly couple over the rail.

They had to have been in their eighties, at least. The woman had one hand on the rail, the other arm hooked through her husband's as they walked calmly toward the ferry. They snapped their heads toward Paul with an offended scowl at his sudden intrusion, but showed no fear, no panic whatsoever.

And it was clear why. The lights from the ferry flooded the rear deck, lighting the aft weather deck like it was high noon on a cloudless day. Paul spun to look behind at the yacht. It was dark, but only for a moment before the lights flickered once, then kicked back on. The crew was even better than Paul had thought. They'd gotten the lights back on in thirty seconds.

He spotted Paloma near the salon entrance, arms crossed, watching the crowd, barely a glance at the lights as they came to life around her, bathed her in an angelic glow. Melantha didn't even bother to glance around, just kept bored eyes on the crowd as it thinned across the bridge to the ferry.

His mind finally catching up to his circumstances, Paul pulled off his glasses and tucked them inside his jacket before Paloma or Melantha could spot him with them on, then pulled off his headphones, holding them at his side. He casually tossed them down the stairs he'd just ascended and fell into step behind the elderly couple.

He watched Melantha scan the crowd, then catch his eye. A slight smile played at the corner of her lips. Those gorgeous, full lips, still painted dark red, as perfect as the moment he'd met her on the ferry. She smiled a bit wider, as if she could read Paul's thoughts, then looked away again.

Paul pulled his thoughts back to what he was doing, then cursed himself. He still hadn't located Stratham, and now he couldn't risk putting the glasses back on. He couldn't risk being spotted wearing highly secret, highly sophisticated prototype tech hardware in public. Especially among this crowd. Odds were that someone here would know what they were, or could guess easily enough that they were worth a fortune in future profits.

Turned out he didn't need to worry. As he shuffled along

behind the elderly couple, in step with the tail end of the crowd, and turned the corner to cross the bridge, he found Stratham. He had his laptop in his hand. He was chatting with a couple of guests.

Already on the ferry.

The wobble of the floating bridge wasn't the only reason Paul's knees felt unsteady as he stepped across. Plan A was officially a bust.

And Paul had no Plan B.

38

THE FERRY CRUISED away from the yacht and pointed toward land, the chatter of the guests much more subdued than it had been earlier that evening. Many stood in pairs, couples talking quietly with each other or just standing at the rail, shoulders slouched and eyes bagged, watching dull-eyed as they approached the marina and the lights of the shoreline grew larger.

But some of the guests were still active, moving around, touching elbows and initiating new conversations. Stratham was one of these. Paul shadowed him, never letting him out of sight, never letting him get more than two or three arm's lengths away as Stratham worked the crowd some more, tireless in his efforts for his boss. Paul could see why someone with presidential ambition like the Attorney General, the front-runner for the Democratic nomination in most people's minds, would hire a man like Stratham. He was good at his job. Even from just one night of observation, Paul could see that.

Which would make his laptop even harder to steal. Stratham still clutched it in his hands, occasionally opening it while speaking to a guest, presumably to record yet another contribution. His empty laptop bag was slung over his shoulder. That wouldn't be easy to steal, either. Stratham had slung the strap across his chest and under his suit jacket. No-Plan B wasn't looking much better than Failed-Plan A. Paul would have to get to the laptop before Stratham put it in his case.

And time was running out. They had just passed the breakwater of the marina. The full-throated outrage of the ferry's engines slowed to a principled indignance, then to a recalcitrant rumble. The guests moved slowly and quietly, gathering at the rail on one side. Even the more active guests grew quiet as the lights of the marina cast yellow shadows over them and the lines of the long pier came into view.

Finally ending his work for the evening, Stratham moved with them. He stood alone at the back of the crowd, holding his laptop open on one palm while he typed with the other hand. If Paul were ever to have a chance, this was it. He moved in close behind Stratham, his fingers itching to touch the metal of the laptop. He could picture it in his mind, could feel its warm weight tucked against his side, held beneath his tuxedo jacket.

But how could he steal the laptop and get away? Stratham would know it had been stolen, of course, and would know Paul had taken it. There could be no subtlety. Paul would have to fight through the waiting crowd, fight through a narrow opening in the rail, then down a long pier with only one exit. Police would already be waiting on shore, summoned by Whitley to guard the pier in the night. Stratham need only shout once or twice to alarm the crowd and alert the cops and Paul would be caught.

Or Paul could subdue Stratham somehow. Knock him out or toss him over the side of the ferry. But someone in the crowd would surely see or hear, would raise the alarm, bring the cops running, and Paul would be caught.

And his whole plan—his larger plan—would be over.

The itch in his fingers faded as the ferry slid along the pier, slowed, and stopped. He heard the shouts of the crew and the soft thumps and scrapes of thick ropes being tossed and tied.

Paul's shoulders slumped as Stratham snapped the laptop shut and slid it into his bag.

"I don't know what game you're playing, Mr. Baker," said Stratham, his back still turned toward Paul.

Paul jerked upright, stock still, his mouth opening and closing like a dying fish.

Stratham turned to face him, his expression placid, hands clasped calmly in front of him. "You've been following me like a toddler since we boarded the ferry. Is there something I can help you with?"

Paul's mouth continued to flap as his mind scrambled to find purchase, to find something plausible to say to explain his behavior.

"Melantha," he spluttered.

Stratham's eyebrows lifted. His eyes shined. "What about her?"

"You two..." Paul was improvising, and not very well. "You seemed to have some kind of history."

"Did we?"

The guests began to file onto the pier. Stratham and Paul followed slowly.

Stratham sighed. "We were together," he said, "for a time." He glanced at Paul, then laughed. "Don't look so surprised, Mr. Baker. Despite what Mrs. Minsk claims, I can be charming." He shrugged. "When it's warranted."

"Why did you break up?" Paul's mouth was making sounds of its own accord, unconnected with his reeling brain.

Stratham gave a forlorn smile, his eyes distant. "Our lives just weren't compatible," he said.

He considered Paul for a moment, then stopped. Paul stopped with him. The two of them stood alone on the pier while the crowd shuffled on without them.

"You slept with her," he said. He tilted his head, eyes narrowing. "Or, rather, I'm guessing that she slept with you."

Paul didn't respond, didn't know how he should respond.

Something in either the look on Paul's face or the squirm in his stance must have told Stratham all he needed to know. Stratham nodded, long and slow, as if everything now made sense to him.

"I'm the last person to give relationship advice, Mr. Baker," he said, resuming his slow stroll down the pier toward the exit. "I'm married to my job, my career." He looked across the water into the night and released a weary sigh. "Maybe even to my candidate." He focused on Paul again. "Melantha is a gorgeous woman, strong and intelligent. But she's also driven, and will not let anything or anyone get in the way of what she wants." Stratham smiled faintly to himself. "We have that in common. Great for a career. Not so great for a relationship."

Paul nodded slowly, trying to understand. "So I shouldn't try to be with her?"

Stratham laughed, a short melody surprisingly low and musical. "You can try all you want. You'll be with her if—and only if—she wants you to be with her."

Paul must have looked confused, for a sympathetic expression came over Stratham's face. "Just don't get too attached," he said. "She can be cruel. Unwittingly, I think, but still cruel, even with those she claims to love." His smile was wry, rueful. "Or to like, at least."

Paul watched, a small voice inside crying out in anguish as Stratham realized his shoulder bag was still open, zipped it shut, and buckled the flap over the top. In his mind, Paul could hear a heavy sound like a prison cell clanging shut, the locks sliding into place with all the menace of a cocking gun.

He let out a deep breath, let out his frustration, his tension. He did his best to let the evening wind coming in off the ocean carry it away. There would be other opportunities to get what he needed. He would have to make sure there were other opportunities. In that case, he was like Melantha. Nothing would get in his way.

And there would be other women. He'd only met Melantha that night. There was no reason for him to obsess over what could have been. It was a fantasy. The last thing Paul needed was to lose himself in fantasy. He needed to stay focused on reality, on the present moment. At least until his work was done.

He and Stratham followed the crowd off the ferry and down the pier, the wood slats shifting and knocking under the parade of expensive shoes. The wind was cool and comfortable, the night sky clear and cloudless above the lights of the city.

Paul felt a slash through his heart when he spied two uniformed police officers standing at the gate at the end of the pier. A slash not of fear, but of heightened awareness, of alertness. You could call it excitement, even. There was still a chance that things could go wrong for him, that Stratham would call Paul's bluff, or that the captain or Paloma would have radioed in from the yacht for the police to arrest Paul and detain him for questioning.

Paul kept his voice low, leaned in toward Stratham. "Tell me," he said, "why did you order a hit on Minsk?"

A slow, sly smile spread over Stratham's face as he slid his eyes from the police officers up ahead to Paul and back. The man missed nothing. He knew a hint when he heard one.

Not a hint. A reminder. A reminder of their detente. Mutually assured destruction.

"I would challenge you to prove that I did, Mr. Baker," Stratham said quietly, neither his ambling gait nor his amused expression wavering in the slightest. "But I can speak hypothetically. In politics, allies are formed, and enemies. And sometimes one can become the other in the blink of a news cycle."

"And when they do, they need to be eliminated?"

"Not unlike arms dealing, or, indeed,"—he gestured to Paul, eyebrows raised—"investing, is it?" Paul kept his expression neutral. Stratham's smile broadened. "Not unlike other endeavors, politics can be a rough business." He returned his gaze forward as they approached the end of the pier. "Or so I'm told."

Paul kept his composure, nodded politely and smiled in a tired, passing way at the police. They paid him no interest at all. Stratham, for his part, didn't even glance at the cops.

A long row of limousines and expensive vehicles with tinted windows had mostly dispersed outside the gate. The guests had separated to their cars and folded inside doors held open for them, then ridden into the night, back to their modern-day palaces. By the time Paul and Stratham made it to the sidewalk, only a handful of rides remained. Paul saw his driver, Jack, standing beside his Cadillac Escalade, still looking fresh, straight-backed and sharp in his black suit and necktie.

Stratham turned to Paul and held out his hand.

"Thank you for an interesting evening," he said as they shook hands. Paul nodded and turned to go, releasing his grip.

But Stratham didn't let go. Paul turned back to him.

"I don't know who you are," Stratham said.

"I'm Paul Ba—"

"I know you're not Paul Baker." Stratham smiled without kindness, baring his teeth. "I know every donor on that yacht, inside and out. I know their ages and birthdays. I know the ages and birthdays of their children, grandchildren, and great-grandchildren. I know the dress size of their wives, the cut of diamond their mistresses prefer. I know their favorite flower, their favorite chocolates, their favorite whiskey. I know everything there is to know about them, because people like that want to feel special. Above all else, they want to feel like they are important."

Paul remembered what Paloma had told him on the deck outside her salon earlier in the evening. "They lack self-respect," he murmured.

Stratham tilted his head. The yellow light from the sodium lamp overhead cut a knife-sharp shadow through one side of his face, sallowed the rest. It gleamed from his eyeglasses. He looked like a villain from an old James Bond film. Paul half-expected a trap door to open beneath his feet and drop him into a pool of ravenous sharks.

"Yes, that's right," Stratham said. He narrowed his eyes at Paul. "But you don't," he said, his voice almost a murmur. Stratham tightened his grip, stepped closer to Paul. His voice was low and soft and eerie. It carried the faint shadow of dark menace. "I don't know who you are, Mr. Baker, but you're not like the rest. You're looking for something else, something entirely different."

Stratham's grip was crushing, surprisingly strong for such a lean, studious-looking man. Perhaps there was more to Stratham than there seemed to be. Maybe the image he presented on the surface was just a role he played, a persona he adopted to make him more effective at his job.

Stratham considered Paul through those narrowed eyes for another long moment. The reflection in his glasses obscured part of one eye. One-eyed in that yellow knife-light, his intense stare seemed inhuman, robotic.

The two police officers got in their cruiser and pulled away, no doubt glad to be done babysitting the rich people. The cool wind gusted, blowing Paul's jacket tight against his back.

As quickly as the gust of wind had come up, it eased. So did Stratham's grip and his gaze. He stood back a step, still holding Paul's hand. The reflection shifted, revealing both of Stratham's eyes again. His stare was more human, but no less intense.

"I don't know what you're looking for, Mr... Baker." The intensity softened. Stratham dropped his chin and gave Paul a knowing look over the top of his glasses. "And I don't know if I want you to find it or not."

After one more long look, Stratham seemed to arrive at some kind of decision. "But I do wish you well," he said. He gave Paul's hand a final pump and released him, turned and walked to his car. His driver held the door open and Stratham got in without looking back. Paul watched the car drive away, watched the red tail lights glare back at him as the car drove out of the marina and into the darkness.

Leaving Paul alone on the dock in the night under the knife edge of the yellow overhead light.

39

THE TAP of his tuxedo shoes rang in the empty night like the ticking of a clock as Paul moved toward his car. Jack held the door open and Paul slid inside, right back to where he'd started just a few hours earlier. The cool black leather seats, the cavernous backseat. Like a prison transport.

Only now he didn't need to be Paul Baker any more. Paul Baker had failed. He could become Cameron Hauk again.

And he wasn't in a prison transport. But his mother was still in her prison cell, and Cameron was no closer to getting her out.

Cam let out a heavy sigh and leaned his head against the window stanchion. From the corner of his eye, he saw Jack flick a glance in the rearview mirror. Cam ignored it, closed his eyes and focused on his breath, extended his senses. He could feel the soft leather of the stanchion against his temple. He could feel the coolness of the window beside his face. He felt the soft swaying as Jack wound through the parking lot and navigated the surface streets toward the freeway, felt himself shift slightly on the smooth leather seats with each movement.

He'd failed that night. It was a setback. But he'd escaped with his freedom. Things could have been much, much worse. He still had a chance to free his mother. Had things gone another way that evening, he could be in a cell himself, with no chance for either of them to taste freedom ever again.

He would find another way. He wouldn't rest until he'd found another way. Stealing Minsk's data had been a bust, but Cam had learned that his intuitions were valid. Like every politician, it seemed, there was something about Attorney General Jenkins' donors that was incriminating. Otherwise, why would Stratham be willing to have Minsk killed? The money was always tainted, always dirty. Cam would just need to find another way to find out exactly how.

He remembered the thumb drive, with the random files he'd copied from Minsk's file system. It was a long shot, a very long shot, but Cam was back to square one again. Even a long shot might yield something he could use. Some evidence, or at least a clue to what his next step could be.

Cam reached into his jacket pocket, felt the thumb drive there. He felt something else and pulled it out.

Stratham's ID.

The soft black lanyard draped over the back of Cam's hand. Cam turned the ID over. There was a message there.

~

If found, drop in mailbox. Return postage guaranteed.
U.S. Department of Justice
950 Pennsylvania Avenue, NW
Washington, D.C. 20530-0001

~

The address of the Office of the Attorney General of the United States.

The office of Attorney General William Jenkins.

Cam turned the card over in his hands. It was thick, rigid,

tough. Thicker and tougher than a typical ID card. Three times as thick as a driver's license. What if it was more than an ID? What if it was a key card?

What if Cam had stolen Stratham's key to the AG's offices?

He slid the card back in his jacket pocket, glanced in the rearview mirror. Jack was watching the road, his eyes attentive and focused on his driving. The freeway was still busy, even at this hour.

Cam leaned his head against the window stanchion again, stared out at the darkness as the buildings lit in the distance drifted by.

Only this time, it wasn't failure he was feeling.

It was hope.

40

Halfway up the Hudson river between Manhattan and Albany, Taconic Correctional Facility in Westchester County, New York was just a few hours from the Catskill Mountains and a pistol shot from the mansions and tennis clubs in Bedford. After driving through the lush fields and forests along the Saw Mill, Cam always found it jarring to see the harsh concrete and razor wire of the prison jut from the pastoral beauty of the surroundings.

Under the washed-out blue sky of that hot, muggy day in late August, Cam felt the same thing again. Only this time, he was buoyed by the hope that he wouldn't be making that trip too much longer. Of course, he'd been carrying that hope for the last fifteen years, but he refused to release it. He would not stop until his mother was free. They had a plan. It was still working. Cam would see it through to the end.

Cam's mother, Paulie Hauk, was already seated at one of the round, orange-coated metal tables in Fishkill's visitation room as Cam endured his fourth frisking since he'd walked through the prison gate. Sue, the sharp-humored guard who did the honors, resembled the horehound candies she loved—dark and round.

And she was just as sweet as the candy, once you looked beneath the tough, acerbic prison guard exterior.

Cam made sure to keep Sue well-stocked with horehound, bringing her a fresh bag every two weeks or so. It was more than just greasing the guards. Sue and the other guards at Fishkill seemed to have a genuine affection for his mother. They watched out for her, spent time talking and laughing with her. Paulie was the kind of person that was hard not to love, but prison guards weren't known as the most affectionate group of people in the world. Cam knew that their attention, their humanity, made Paulie's life in prison more bearable. For that kindness, Cam would bring them all the horehound candies in the world and still consider his debt unpaid.

He sat down opposite his mother, the hard surface of the quarter-round bench uncomfortable against his tailbone. He opened his hand, curled his middle and ring fingers down to his palm, and pressed it flat against the table. His mother did the same, their fingertips mere inches from each other.

The gesture was American Sign Language for *I love you*. It was their ritual greeting when Cam visited. Visitations were allowed twice a week on Sunday and Thursday. Cam came every weekend, unless he was away on a job. Physical contact with prisoners was strictly forbidden, so they pressed their hands on the table and kept their fingertips inches apart. As much as Cam wanted to wrap his mother in a bear hug, he would not risk revocation of her visitation rights for a brief moment of joy.

He and his mother were playing a much longer game, one that would earn his mother her freedom forever.

"How was your summer vacation?" Paulie asked. Her jet-black hair was shiny and smooth and shot through with streaks of silver, giving Paulie a rock-star aura. She'd been salt-and-pepper for as long as Cam could remember, but the salt did seem to have gained on the pepper in the last few years. That, plus the shadows beneath her eyes that seemed to grow darker and deeper with each passing year, made Cam's jaw muscles clench. "Was it everything you'd hoped?"

Prison visits were often recorded, so Cam and Paulie had to speak in code. Criminals did have some rights, but privacy was not one of them. He and his mother spoke in the code they'd used Cam's whole life. When you robbed people and institutions for a living, it helped to be able to communicate openly without clueing people in to your true intentions. A robbery was the same as any other endeavor, with goals and milestones, sub-objectives, tools, obstacles, etc. You could speak about anything. As long as the other person knew what the real objective was, they could translate the code well enough. And Cam and his mother had spent a lifetime perfecting the code. By now, they barely needed to speak at all. They could practically read each other's minds.

"It didn't go quite the way I expected," Cam said. His mother arched one eyebrow. Her pale blue eyes seemed to glow like arctic ice against her dark hair, set off even more by the dark semi-circles under her eyes. "But it was a good break, all the same. California is beautiful in the summertime."

Paulie smiled and sighed. "I remember," she said wistfully. "Your father and I spent a lot of time out West." Her smile brightened. "Do you remember that summer we spent in Monterey?"

Cam nodded. When he was nine or ten, his parents had robbed a county bank in Carmel. They'd spent the summer before the job living in a tiny beach rental in Monterey while they cased the bank, gathered their team, and made all the preparations for the bank hit.

"You dove right into the ocean on that first day, thinking it would be warm like the Carolinas." She snickered. "You came back out of there so fast you were practically walking on water."

Paulie's eyes pinched shut as she laughed, ringing loud and clear and musical off of the concrete walls. Two other inmates had visitors at the same time, conversing in hushed murmurs around the room. They and the lone guard in the far corner turned to look at Paulie as she laughed. They couldn't help but smile with her.

Cam chuckled too. He still remembered how icy the water had been. The shock was as much a blow to his mind as to his body. A lesson in the danger of preconceptions. He'd gone back in later, but not until the heat of the day had him sweating like a beast, when he'd known what to expect and the icy-cold sea had been a relief, not a shock.

"Did you get out on the water at all this time?" Paulie asked.

She knew he had. They'd made the plan together, as much as they could while speaking in riddles in the middle of a prison.

Cam nodded. "I did, actually," he said. "It wasn't quite what I expected, but I'd still call it a rewarding experience."

Melantha's face came to his mind unbidden. He frowned slightly.

"Oh, dear," said Paulie, "I know that look." Her voice was soft and warm. It was as close to a mother's embrace as Cam had been able to come in the last fifteen years. He clung to it, a paltry surrogate for his mother's arms. "What was her name?"

Cam sniffed a laugh. His mother knew him better than anyone in the world. She was his best friend, the only one who could begin to understand him. And Cam was beginning to think it would always be that way.

If such a thing as soulmates existed, his parents had been it. They'd given Cam a childhood filled with love and laughter. And, yes, crime, too. But they'd always taught Cam that the theft of money and jewels was just a redistribution of wealth. In a way, it was furthering the meritocracy that America had always pretended to be.

They never stole from anyone who couldn't afford the loss. Banks and billionaires, not bus drivers or businesspeople with young families. And they were staunchly opposed to even the threat of violence. Cam's parents had a stronger moral code that most of the thugs on Wall Street that were heralded as the success stories of the time. For Cam, those people were marks, not role models.

Given his parents' abhorrence of violence, the accidental death of his father, caught in the crossfire of a bank robbery he wasn't involved in, was beyond ironic. It was the gut punch of a universe that seemed to side with the Wall Street thugs. Cam had watched, stunned, from the car window as his mother wept on the sidewalk and his father died in her arms. She had barely seemed to notice as the cops figured out who she was and arrested at the scene. She and Cam had spent the fifteen years since working tirelessly to find a way to get her out of prison.

Cam's history came from pretty unique circumstances, not the kind of thing you could explain on a first date or even a twenty-first date. No wonder Cam had such a hard time finding a woman to be with.

"Her name was Melantha," he said, his voice small and quiet. "But it was nothing."

"Not nothing," said his mother in that same embracing tone. "I can see that much."

Cam felt tears well in his eyes, laughed bitterly, and looked to the ceiling, as much to roll his eyes at himself as to push the tears back down. "It should be nothing," he whispered. "I barely even knew her."

"Sometimes you don't need to," Paulie whispered.

"Like you and dad."

Paulie nodded and let out a heavy sigh. "You'll find your love someday, Cam," she said.

Cam smiled weakly at his mother. He was starting to doubt that would ever be true.

But that wasn't important. "I'll tell you what I did find," he said, lowering his voice and forcing himself to ignore the urge to glance around to make sure the guard wasn't looking. There was nothing more suspicious than someone looking over their shoulder.

"There's a class that's offered every year," he said, "but it's very hard to get into. Admission is very selective. I figured I'd never get in, so I was looking for other ways to strengthen my resume, make sure I could stay at the top of the class."

Cam was entering his senior year as a criminology student at Attorney General Jenkins' alma mater. Jenkins had long been a sponsor of the school, increasing the visibility of his sponsorship as his own career advanced. As Attorney General, he made a point to take each year's top five graduates to dinner in a private room at a tony restaurant in downtown D.C., granting them an audience with the AG himself to seek advice or wheedle a job offer.

And for the valedictorian each year, in addition to the dinner, he would grant them a private audience, several hours hanging out with the Attorney General of the United States. A rare opportunity. Over the years, he'd taken several of the students under his wing and launched them into promising careers of their own. All while making the AG seem like a true humanitarian, of course. Helps the presidential credentials.

Cam needed that private audience. His entire plan depended on it.

"Turns out there is an opening for the class after all," Cam continued. "If I can get in and do well, that should give me what I need to cinch the top spot."

Paulie nodded slowly. "Sounds like a tough class," she said. "Lots of competition, and you're top of your class right now. Is there any risk it could hurt your GPA?"

Cam shrugged. "There's always a risk," he said. "You know that." He grinned at his mother. "But I'm a hell of a good student."

Paulie grinned back at him. "You always have been."

"I think it's worth the risk."

Paulie's grin softened to a wistful smile. "You know, Cam, it's okay if you don't finish at the top of your class. You can still have a wonderful career without being valedictorian."

Cam considered what the rest of his life would be like with his mother stuck in prison. He knew she was trying to give him an out, to set him free from any obligation he felt to secure her release.

But it wasn't obligation that drove Cam. He simply couldn't imagine life without his mother. As unlikely as it seemed, what if he did find love? Would he get married without his mother at the wedding? Have children who never knew their grandmother, who could never sit in their arms while she read them a book or told them a story or showed them how to pick a lock? The thought made him sick to his stomach. Life without his mother in it—on the outside, free—was not a full life. He was working to free her as much for himself as for her.

"I know, mom," he said. God, he wished he could put his arm around her or at least hold her hand, to reassure her with his touch. Instead, he hoped his voice and the look in his eyes would be enough. "It just wouldn't be the same. For me."

Paulie searched his eyes for a long moment. Her own eyes filled with water, the pale blue shimmering. She smiled again, warm and full and genuine.

"Okay," she whispered. "Okay."

She wiped her eyes with one finger, glanced up at the guard and gave him a sheepish look. Cam glanced over to see him smiling back at Paulie, a genuine look of compassion.

All the candy in the world wouldn't even make a dent.

"Now," Paulie said, sniffing once and setting both hands carefully on the table in front of her. She looked up at Cam with a devilish grin. "Tell me about this girl."

~

As Cam drove, winding away from the concrete and razor wire through the lush fields and forests, easing his car around the gentle curves toward the river, toward the highway, and back toward Washington, he felt the usual mix of emotion. His heart was full from seeing his mother, tears an eyelash-breadth away from his eyes. But that same fullness brought pain to his chest. His heart chafed against the bars of his ribs, resenting its confinement.

Tears wouldn't solve anything. Pain wouldn't help. But it did bring him focus.

Focus and resolve.

He resisted the urge to stomp on the accelerator, to speed as fast as his used Nissan would go. Back to D.C., back to school. Back to the plan. Getting pulled over for speeding would help nothing at all.

One year left. One year of school, of work, of deception. And then he could finally confront the Attorney General and make his play.

Cam had to make sure the play succeeded. If it didn't, there would be no second chance. If Cam failed, both he and his mother would be in jail for the rest of their lives.

The soft grip of the steering wheel crackled as Cam clenched his hands. All of that pain, all of that emotion, all of that energy. He poured it all into a singular focus on a specific goal.

His mother's freedom.

That was all that mattered.

After a few miles, the emotion settled. The pain in his chest eased. Cameron's grip on the steering wheel loosened.

But his focus never wavered.

ACKNOWLEDGMENTS

As always, my love and thanks to Holly. Without your support, my love, none of this would be possible.

ABOUT THE AUTHOR

Kevin Robert Aldrich lives in California and is the author of several mystery and romance novels:

If you love a twisting, pulse-pounding mystery, you'll love Eyes in the Dark and Key Witness.

If you love heart-pounding romantic suspense, you'll love Bare Trap and Flames of Freedom.

If you like vampires, witches, and forbidden love, get a copy of Spellbound now.

And if you love powerful contemporary romance, try Racing Hearts and Ollie & Alli today.

MORE FROM THE AUTHOR

To learn more about Kevin Robert Aldrich and stay up-to-date with all of his stories and novels, please visit his website:

www.kevinrobertaldrich.com

To be automatically notified of every new release, join the Kevin Robert Aldrich mailing list at the website above.